Ten tales of horror and dark fantasy, each with the retro–vintage flair readers have come to appreciate from the Curiosities anthology series.

A poet makes a passage with death. A solitary monster meets another. Nazi war experiments run amuck on the Eastern Front. Unsettling sounds follow you through the New England woods. A sea captain takes in a mermaid, though it may be his doom. One very monstrous clock. And more.

From the gothic to the grotesque, these exhibits will have you trading your steampunk browns for gothic blacks, and back again.

Featuring a guest editorial on the roots of cosmic horror by the queen herself, Mary SanGiovanni.

"Appointment in Time" ©2012 by James Dorr, first appeared in
        Years End: 14 Tales of Holiday Horror (Untreed Reads).
"Curio" ©2021 by Catherine McCarthy.
"The Curse of the Thorn" ©2017 by Elaine Vilar Madruga,
        English translation ©2021 by Toshiya Kamei.
"A Dog's Death" ©2021 by Diana A. Hart.
"The Monstrous Metronome" ©2021 by Lena Ng.
"Lovecraft's Legacy of Cosmic Horror" ©2021 by Mary SanGiovanni.
"The Peculiarity of Two" ©2021 by Liam Hogan.
"The Revellers" ©2021 by Marisca Pichette.
"Silvergloom" ©2021 by Jonathan Louis Duckworth.
"To Our Own Ghosts" ©2021 by Deborah L. Davitt.
"The Well-Trained Thing in Constance's Dress" ©2019 by John
        Adams, first appeared in *Siren's Call*, October 2019.

Cover Art: "The Little Mermaid" by Bogdan Marica.

Edited by Kevin Frost and Andrew McCurdy
Book Design & Layout by Kevin Frost in
Tres Piedras, New Mexico

ISBN: 978-1-948396-14-1 (Print on Demand)

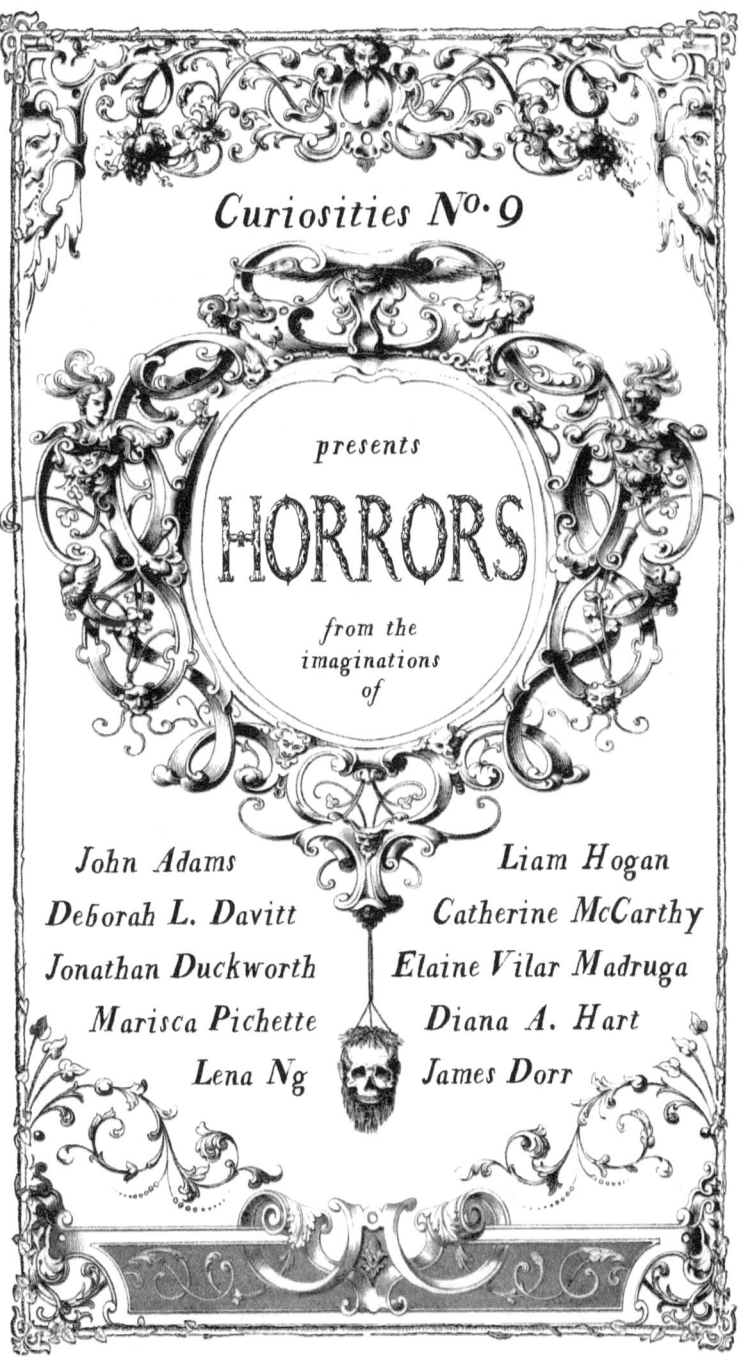

Curiosities No. 9

presents

HORRORS

from the
imaginations
of

John Adams

Deborah L. Davitt

Jonathan Duckworth

Marisca Pichette

Lena Ng

Liam Hogan

Catherine McCarthy

Elaine Vilar Madruga

Diana A. Hart

James Dorr

THE HORRORS

⟶fiction⟵

There's a saying amongst the steampunks: there is no steampunk music—there is music that steampunks like. I suppose the same could be said for steampunk horror. While steampunk is not a horror subgenre, there is definitely a type of horror that steampunks like. It's hard to define, but you know it when you're near it.

There must be a nod towards our gothic forerunners, with all their black and purple finery faded to shades of brown and russet. Whether a manor ghost or an anxious protagonist of delicate nerves, we must have a proper sense of dread.

The macabre is bound to get seedy around the edges. Body modification. Side shows. Questionable taxidermy exhibits. Romanceable drug habits. We've all indulged.

There will be crowd pleasers, of course. One of the classic Universal monsters is bound to appear, or perhaps we will cross paths with Death as they patiently stalk their next appointment. We could have a fairy tale too, deconstructed and remade to order. And if things don't go well, the Devil is always ready to make a deal.

Has H.P. Lovecraft been mentioned yet? It does not have to be tentacles or deranged cultists, but there is no possible way I would be able to assemble a set of stories like this without someone bringing the old boy up.

For the history majors amongst us, there must always be a war story. It is just the way it is. Where you have steampunks you will have at least one history major and they will loudly demand a war story.

And there must be texture. Always lush textures. Blood is never going to come out of that historically accurate hand-stitched brushed velvet Californio jacket with matching gear-encrusted bison leather tool belt, but one does not enter a dissection laboratory poorly equipped.

"But wait," I hear the cry from the horror side of the aisle. *"That's not horror at all. That's dark fantasy!"*

And they might be right, so let's humor them. What would real steampunk horror look like? I suppose that would be the one where our plucky protags, armed with all their tech savvy, rebellious youth, and item of singular hardware, are seduced by their own hubris and become dystopian overlords.

You won't find *that* story in this volume.

But as for the rest? Come inside and see.

Kevin Frost
Tres Piedras, New Mexico
December 2021

Elaine Vilar Madruga
translated by Toshiya Kamei

The Curse of
the Thorn

 O YOU WANT ME TO FESS UP, Lis? Mea culpa? Guilty as charged. I transformed your body. Sacrificed your mother. My harpoon slipped out of my hand before I'd realized you were covered by her cries and scales. No amount of forgiveness will absolve me. My hands are forever stained with the blood of the woman who gave you life.

Still, her revenge came galloping years later, when we thought we were safe. Only fools believe love conquers all.

Do you want my confession? You're your mother's revenge—a harpoon plunging deep into my spine with all her smiles.

Yes, there's no denying it. There's only one culprit. Not her, nor you.

~~~

Cycle 8, ijnno dossi year

Yesterday I left terra firma. Puerto Escara gradually grew smaller along with the steamboats, the magic of the solipdists, and the laughter of children who had gathered on the docks to see us off. A santacantaora soared through the air above the masts leaving smoke trails, signs of good luck.

Then, it was the sea.

For a long time, I hadn't felt so alive. The years spent away from the sea had left deep scars on my psyche. I shouldn't have fooled myself into thinking that my seafaring days were behind me. Today, the *Neuf* is mine. I recall the joy I'd felt years ago, when I was a stowaway in a vessel traversing the waters.

The first war remains vivid in my memory. Five years without setting foot on terra firma. Such a long absence made me resent words such as sea, seaweed, length, mainmast, sentry, knots, and, above all, that damn alarm call piercing the nights: sirens. They were to blame for keeping us away from the port. For forcing us to fight for control over maritime routes and fishing. For preventing us from paying the tithe our king demanded.

Ten years of war. And the same old painful price to pay. Dead sailors. Our navigator lost his mind when he learned a gigantic wave had finished off his fishing village and swallowed his wife and their newborn daughter. Hunger. Starvation. The cities supplied us little fuel. After curfew time, it was too risky to navigate the ship in the artificial mist the sirens spewed. The danger could be mitigated if the ship had a cryo-vapor reserve to fly over the waters. Yet, paranoia spread far and wide, and many ships suffered friendly fire. The same excuses were repeated again and again. No way to tell who was responsible because anything could be attributed to the sirens' deception in the mist.

Their songs would inspire suicidal thoughts and murderous wishes. They offered us poisoned shells, which some madmen still picked up when they got tangled up in the nets, hoping to find a pearl, a treasure, or any other wonder that would wipe away the poverties of the sea and war. We soon stopped eating rotten fish. Siege. Blockade. Men drowned under the moonlight when nobody else was on the lookout. Alleged accidents.

We had trouble hunting the wretched sirens. They swam in pods. Attacked en masse. Killing machines. Those scaled torpedoes traveled beneath the surface until they spotted the weakest point in their foe's defenses. Silent guerrillas hovering underwater.

In those years, I rarely had a good night's sleep. Insomnia was my faithful companion. I could sleep only when the navigator turned on the cryo-vapor engines so that the ship would rise in the air, out of the sirens' reach. Paranoia bred more paranoia. The cryo-vapor was consumed at a faster rate than bread. A few hours of peaceful sleep over the deceptive waters.

<p style="text-align:center">~~~</p>

Cycle 11, ijnno dossi year

We hunted the sirens with nets and harpoons. What a wretched task it was. At times, we hurled bombs into the water, with hopes that they would land on a pod below the surface. We almost always missed our targets.

Then one day, Lady Luck smiled on us. A lone siren swam by herself, perhaps in search of some trinket newbie sailors traded for rusty gold from sunken ships.

It was the navigator who threw his harpoon. He hadn't quite lost his wits. His aim was dead-on. He had an enviable view of the creature, basking like a sea lion. He was in luck, no doubt. The siren had forgotten to cover her vulnerable scaled tail with iron meshes. The navigator skewered her cleanly.

I'll never forget her screams as long as I live. The water was tinged with blood. The fish girl kept wiggling as she became more entangled in the net. We hurled her onto the deck. One blow after another landed on her. Her shrieks pierced our ears once again. The sailors' screams. Kicks. She pleaded for her life in her screeching language.

The navigator looked for her belly. He snickered when, out of reflex, she covered herself with her scaled hands, which were hard and crystalline. A brutal blow struck her head. The gills on her naked torso trembled. She gasped for air. The scales on her belly had turned blue.

The navigator stabbed his harpoon into her, once, twice, then a third time.

One of my men quipped, "Let's have her for dinner. There's no better feast." Then we all giggled and guffawed until our sides ached.

~~~

Cycle 12, ijnno dossi year

They called it the curse of the thorn.

On terra firma, I consulted the best wizards and medcs, hoping to hear something different from the words I'd already heard: "Nothing can be done." It was her fault. The lone siren we gobbled down that night like gluttonous children at a birthday party. I could still taste her in my mouth.

Yes, of course.

Over the course of the next twenty rotations of the sun, the sailors began to suffer mysterious ailments. Some saw their legs and arms shrivel like plants wilting in the scorching sun. In a few years, they'd become beggars, pleading for alms in Puerto Escara. Most of the men, however, suffered internal organ failures: heart, lungs, and stomach. They agonized on the ship's deck, confined in trembling piles waiting for the outcome, the remoteness of the pain. On many occasions, I felt an urge to harp them to end their groans, screams, and tears once and for all.

Me? Unlike many others, I suffered only a small misfortune. To be precise, my seed dried up. I was doomed to sterility and death. Over the years, countless wizards and medcs had examined my body, offered me their prayers, and poked me all over my body. Yet, all gave me the same answer: "Nothing can be done."

It's the gods' will. The curse of the thorn traveled with me and my manhood shriveled up to nothing.

～～～

Cycle 20, ijnno dossi year

Who doubts it? Peace is an extremely fragile toy, breakable by the slightest touch. Just breathing on it will cause it to wither, blow away, and crumble.

Fifteen years of peace began with a non-aggression treaty, signed over the massacres on the western sea. Corpses floated on the water. Human legs. Sirens' mangled tails. Fingers and toes. Ripped gills. Broken spears. Poisoned pearls.

Peace and utopia. What nonsense!

With the rank of captain, one less leg, and a war veteran's pension, I left the waters behind. After ten years, during which I saved my wages, I was able to afford a cryo leg cultivated in the medcs' organ gardens. I lived in Puerto Escara, that infamous place that should be swept away from the kingdom. I was an old sea wolf. Eight- and nine-year-old petty thieves —many of them war orphans—would ask me, "What are they like? Is the curse of the thorn true? Did you ever harpoon one of those?"

The *Neuf* wasn't a warship worth my life. Even the poor devils who accompanied me deserved better. She was an old ship, practically useless. Maybe that's why I was assigned as captain. A piece of junk for Eder'ym, a former cripple cursed by the thorn, a veteran of the first war who still dreamed of the sea.

~~~

Do you want me to fess up, Lis?

The night was pitch-dark. The *Neuf* had almost capsized a few hours earlier. My chest filled with hatred against the sirens, but also against the miser king who had granted us only paltry credits to buy cryo-vapor.

We had to sleep on the water like animals at the mercy of a silent predator's fangs. As the old saying goes, big fish eat little fish. It's one of the few that rings utterly true.

Flying at night over the waters is the only way to guarantee safety in this war.

Our ship hovered above the sea while the crew took turns sleeping, haunted by death.

A wave roared toward us. Artificial. Huge. It'd been created to sink the ship. It rose above the *Neuf* and I knew right away: a pod of sirens espied us.

The gods of the sea didn't want me dead, Lis. You must believe me. We'd run out of cryo-vapor. The *Neuf* was too heavy to rise above the waters in time and fly above the wave. I prayed. That mass of dark water approached our flimsy vessel. Just as it was about to swallow us like a shard of barely floating wood, a miracle happened: the wave came to a halt. We were so close that we could reach out our hands and feel its dampness.

Do you want my confession, Lis? I cried. Bawled. The wave moved westward, letting me know that a decisive battle took place there. The horizon took on a reddish glow with fire and death. The dark lump moved on in search of more juicy prey. I breathed a sigh of relief. The sirens would leave along with the wave. My men would have one more night to live.

When dawn broke, I steered the *Neuf* west, in the hope that some ship had survived the chaos on the sea. You don't remember the war, my dear Lis. Neither do you know what I saw. Destruction. Driftwoods. Sirens' corpses. Lumps of petrified scales colliding against the remains of boats. Harpoons. Blood. Bone chips and shrapnel. The shadow of a spell, Lis, had frozen a wave: it stood like a piece of ice, a merciless god's hand above the shattered sea.

I was about to order a retreat when the terrified eyes of my sailors began to sting me like salt in an open wound. Fear of death had penetrated the depths of their souls. Poor helpless boys!

Then I spotted her behind the frozen wave.

Threw my harpoon. *Missed her.* I thought, clicking my tongue in frustration. Then a wound opened in her belly. The harpoon pierced through her and nailed her against the surface of the wave.

She couldn't escape. Her scales had petrified around the harpoon, making it impossible for her to slip through its embrace. The weapon possessed some solipdist spell that kept her from escaping.

She saw us. As she glared at me, she burst into wailing as sirens do when they know their end is near. Those moans sneak into your eardrums and addle your brain. It gets worse by the second.

"Let's take care of the little fishy," I sneered. My cowardly chicks seemed to have been struck by a bolt of courage. "Let's show this little mermaid how much a wave is worth."

Your mother stirred, Lis, my child. My harpoon was her shackle. Do you want the truth? I enjoyed her suffering. I laughed when she struggled, in vain, to slip away. A sneer formed across my face when she spat out blood as her scaled body became petrified. Her eyes locked on mine, and she screeched again.

"Shut up, little fishy."

My sailors began to poke her with harpoons and sticks. One spat at her face.

"Where's the wave that saves you? Where are your friends? Did they leave you behind when they saw you were caught?"

Do you want my confession, Lis? I hated her. Her race had slaughtered my brothers in arms, turned children into thieving orphans at Puerto Escara, and deprived my navigator of his wife and daughter. Her kind had denied me love and pleasure.

"Now you're going to find out what the curse of the harpoon is all about," I said.

She glared at me again, Lis. Begged for mercy. But that word wasn't a part of my vocabulary then. My harpoon pierced her neck at the precise moment her eyes—always her eyes—made one last plea.

Life slipped away from her body. Her petrified scales turned back to crystalline webs.

"Take the harpoon," I told my sailors. Magical weapons were too valuable to be thrown away in war.

One of my men dragged her body and threw it overboard. At the moment, a pair of eyes—yours —stared at me.

You had hidden between your mother's body and the frozen wave. You had no shield. You had no more than three gold declas on your necklace. You still had baby teeth. Your scales hadn't yet learned to petrify. You were alone, next to the two harpoons that had killed your mother. Her body sank. For a moment, you seemed to swim after her, but you didn't, my child. You were too young to know words such as hate, danger, war, massacre, and revenge.

You screamed as like your mother, but it wasn't a call of fear, but of welcome, as if we—murderers —were the members of that pod that had left you with the dying siren. You seemed helpless and small, like many children the sirens drowned in the kingdom's beaches and ports.

Her corpse sank and you didn't escape, Lis. You caught my eye, and revenge—the true curse of the thorn—pierced my heart like the harpoon into your mother.

~~~

Cycle 39, ijnno dossi year

Inside the cabin, at least three times a day—when destroying or disarming the enemy didn't demand my time—I was content to see her. She could breathe outside the fishbowl, but she'd suffocate after a few minutes. I tried to make her speak, but the little mermaid was capricious. She only made her usual sounds.

My men shot me resentful looks. I deserved it. Many were terrified at the idea of having an abominable creature on board that could, at any time, spit mist, create artificial waves or poisonous pearls. They didn't get it, though. She was just a girl.

Was I moved with pity or regret? Beats me. But deserting such a helpless creature in the midst of war seemed a terrible thing to do.

I dispensed so many fibs these days. My men seemed to take my words at face value, but as time went by, their trust crumbled to dust.

"We'll sell her once we get home," I told them. "Any sorcerer or solipdist would pay a fortune for a live siren. Only few get caught and are brought to dry land."

Meanwhile, I dredged the sirens' trinkets and weapons from the flotsam and hoarded them in secret. In Puerto Escara, a few scholars would pay handsome sums for them. Poisonous pearls as large as snake eggs, tridents and blades laden with fish venom, tail fragments, and other junk I could sell in the right places for credits. That was my plan.

And transforming Lis.

This latest war had turned men into cowards. In the previous war, wizards and collectors didn't pay, not even a grubby coin, for any of my spoils. Now, they were rarities, as they hardly ever made it to Puerto Escara. Sailors had become wary of the legends surrounding the sirens' curse and nightly killings. Few men dared snatch secrets from the sea.

I needed to be careful, of course. Unknown objects and garments floated adrift, but I'd never touch them. May the gods protect me.

'Lis' was my great grandmother's name. It's a beautiful name. My dream of having a child had sown its roots in my sterility. Perhaps the gods have answered my prayer, after all.

I needed to turn her into a human being.

~~~~

Cycle 41, ijnno dossi year

Possible? Of course it is. Medcs grow organs in their gardens as if they were fruit hanging on branches. They gave me an artificial leg almost identical to the real one. Wizards cast their spells and performed transmutations.

They will be able to transform her. Make her scales, fins, gills, and tail disappear. She'll be like any other girl. She'll grow up by my side. I'll strive to make her happy. She'll never remember the war or her mother.

Lis, my daughter. I like the sound of that.

~~~

Cycle 53, *ijnno dossi year*

We ran out of bread and water. Cryo-vapor? Don't count on it.

I've requested permission from the *Ura*, the largest ship in the fleet, to reach the nearest port and supply the *Neuf* with the few remaining credits. It's our only hope. But the *Ura* doesn't answer. It may have vanished, like so many other vessels. Or it wanders through the fog the sirens have conjured up, waiting for a rescue that will never come. Who would dare in these times to go through a siege like that! Maybe they're just ignoring my call.

The sea is a disgusting beggar. It demands everything from you without giving back anything in return.

Hunger gnaws at our stomachs. Today, someone proposed we eat Lis's flesh. "She's small, but we can all share a piece." My rage prevented me from speaking. I didn't remind them she was a little girl, a victim of war: it'd have been a waste of my breath. I told them about the curse of the thorn, the men who died as their organs shriveled up, and my ailments. Then the poor devils shuddered at the idea of not being able to hold a woman in the port again.

But Lis is in danger as our hunger grows. The *Ura* ignores my repeated request, the encrypted messages I send. Meanwhile, as a port has come into view, I've made a decision. There was no other choice left. I'll leave the *Neuf* when I reach the mainland, with all my treasures, with my daughter.

Listen, Lis.

The port was called Yugular, one of the poorest in the kingdom. Its coasts had been swept more than thirteen times by pods of sirens that bore their waves against the inhabitants. The authorities never banned landings, although the ship lacked the authorization of the largest ship in the fleet. No one cared about these matters, however. A ship with leprosy, plague, epidemic? You'll be welcomed if you can pay taxes. Renegade sailors fleeing from the king's orders? Ditto, if you pay in advance. Pirates? Smugglers? Criminals? Poverty forces.

Yugular was the right place, perhaps the only place that would receive both of us—a fugitive and an enemy.

Deception had become a part of me: head, stump, limbs, and lies. It became easier to look my men in the eye and say, "Everything will be all right. I've request-ed a landing permit from the customs authorities.

Tomorrow or the day after tomorrow, we'll disembark, but first I must go down alone and talk to the local commander. They aren't used to receiving many foreigners, so they're a bit paranoid.

I'll take care of everything and make them allow us back on solid ground. When I come back tonight, I'll bring tons of food and women in need of some loving. I'll sell the mermaid."

Lis, they believed me. Wretched souls. The *Neuf* was stranded at the entrance to the port. I disem-barked with you and my dunnage, the payment for a life of war that had hatched so many lies. My sailors waved me goodbye with smiles.

"Come back soon, Captain," one of them shouted as I gave him a salute and gently squeezed the fishbowl in my arm. You were inside, my daughter, more valuable than honor and shame.

Why did I love you so much, Lis? So desperately? We were enemies. I could have killed you, and nobody would bat an eye. Maybe it was the curse of the thorn your mother threw at me with her last gaze. I was doomed to raise you and protect you. Or maybe it's just my heart, softened after seeing so much water and blood in this life.

We disembarked, Lis. I paid the tax while rejoic-ing at the fact that you were free from bondage. The *Neuf* soon faded from my memory. We navigated through the labyrinth of streets, garbage cans, and filth, until the sea blurred. The city lay before us, that seedy dump where you'd grow up. Some curious and thieving eyes hovered over us. At first glance, we seemed like easy prey, but my treasures were more terrible than wonderful, Lis. No one dared come near a man cursed by the thorn who carried a mermaid in a fishbowl.

"I need a wizard right now. I'll pay handsomely whoever wants to be my guide," I yelled.

Five volunteers emerged from the street junctions. I chose one, the one who seemed the least dangerous, a one-armed teenager who coughed up blood, undoubtedly consumed prematurely by some disease of the port.

We trod forward, feeling eyes on us, through streets that had lost their names, crossing garbage cans and labyrinthine buildings.

Hope made me let my guard down. Soon you were going to be a healthy, normal girl like any other. People wouldn't remember the man who carried a fishbowl or the mermaid gazing at the streets of Yugular with curiosity.

"Here it is. C'mon, pay me," said the young man, extending his hand to receive payment.

"If you ever tell a living soul about us," I warned, "I swear, I'll cut your heart out. I hate nosy busybodies."

"C'mon, old man. Pay up. My lips are sealed."

"They better be. You know we sea lions can track our prey by the sense of smell." It was a lie, of course, but the look of terror on his face assured me he wasn't going to betray me.

"Thanks, old man," he mumbled. He bowed when I held out one more coin. "Good luck with your fishy there."

He pointed to a wooden door with his only hand.

"Well, old man. Here's the wizard's house."

All he had to do was say his name. The door slid open and a man of indefinite age appeared on the threshold. His wrinkles were visible, but they were smoothed out by holograms, rejuvenation surgeries, spells, and other tricks that maintained his youthful appearance. The stinging odor of formaldehyde and death lingered in the air.

"What have you got there?" he asked, without inviting us in. "Fresh fish for my potions?"

He sneered, baring yellowed teeth like a hyena.

"I've got a few things that might interest you."

I threw my bag of treasures. The wizard amused himself by rummaging inside. I went over my mental inventory. He wanted to rip me off, like all of his kind.

"Well, very good. Yeah, I may be interested. Although this is not...You've got too many pearls. Ah, a solipdist harpoon. Interesting, no?" He glanced at me again. "Let's see, thief, which ship did you rob?"

"Do you want the whole thing?"

"No way, man. These pearls are useless to me. Of course, I must admit it, you've got some interesting... dangerous stuff. I doubt anyone will pay more than eighty credits for a solipdist harpoon. It's—how shall I put it?—unstable."

"You can have all if you transform her." I pointed to your fishbowl, Lis. The wizard widened his eyes.

"The little fishy you've got there? No way. If you sell her to me, I'll pay you three times the amount I promised for the harpoon."

"She's not for sale."

The wizard clucked like an old hen.

"Listen, you thief. Sirens are the worst kind of bitches and give birth to water demons. Haven't you heard of the curse of the thorn? If you eat her, you'll dry up like a rootless tree, you moron."

"Sorry, no deal."

"Hah, hah, hah," he laughed again and tapped me on the shoulder. "So a love of land and sea, huh? It's a good theme for bards, no doubt. You'll have to wait a bit, sailor, if you want a mature mermaid."

I wanted to break his rotten neck, Lis. But I restrained myself.

"Are you good with spells, wizard?"

"I'm the best you can find in Yugular, sailor."

"Have you performed transmutations?"

"Temporary ones, yes. Not permanent ones, though."

He'd read my mind, Lis. He knew I wanted to make you human.

"I'm the best you can find in Yugular, sailor," he repeated. "But don't expect me to turn your abomination into a human girl. Such a thing shouldn't be allowed."

"She's my daughter. I'll do whatever it takes to make her normal."

"Normal? She's exactly what you see, no more, no less—a siren. If you transform her, you'll only distort her. Forget about your so-called daughter and leave her to me. You'll be handsomely compensated."

Do you want me to confess, Lis?

Under my clothes I had hidden the greatest treasures. My instincts told me the wizard wasn't able to reject them. I displayed the merchandise in front of the holograms covering his withered face. Greed, possession, and urgency—signs appearing over his wrinkles.

"How did you get them?"

"They're fertilized," I said. "They'll be yours if you make my daughter human."

I found them floating like buoys on the high seas. Sisters of yours.

"Perfect. I'll do what you say. My best spells, sailor. I'll turn your fish into a girl."

He extended his hands like a beggar.

"But you must know, sailor, that the transmutation isn't permanent."

✄✄✄

Cycle 80, ijnno dossi year

Lis recovered well. We had found shelter in one of the labyrinthine buildings. Our neighbors were eyeless old women, orphaned urchins, folks who had nowhere else to go. They didn't care too much. They thought Lis was one of the countless mutilated victims in war.

The wizard warned as he flashed his cynical grin. "She'll hurt terribly, perhaps for the rest of her life." He split Lis's tail into two, transmuted her, distorted her, and cast his spells on her flesh. My daughter ended up with deformed legs, and passed out from the pain magic couldn't mitigate.

"Does she suffer a lot?" I asked. An oily trace of hypocrisy oozed out of my body. None of that mattered if the charlatan could make my daughter human.

"Bones are the worst," the wizard replied as new bones began to grow inside my daughter's legs. Femurs took shape in her. One bone after another hardened, culminating in the formation of the skeleton. The stench of scorched flesh sizzled up in a thin stream.

Her scars were unsightly, jagging across her body. In each place where a scale grew, a rose window emerged, as if they were smallpox marks. Stretch marks had replaced her gills. The wizard assured me that she'd be able to speak, although never in a clear voice.

I handed him the eggs. Lis became as human as she could be.

"It'll continue to hurt, but as time passes, it'll be tolerable." The wizard said in a slightly upbeat tone, perhaps because he was content with his treasure. "But I must tell you, sailor, the transmutation isn't permanent."

"Don't forget that. Someday her legs will turn back into a tail again, her bones will disappear, her speech will become a screech. Once a siren, always a siren. She'll begin to spew mist and spit out that white phlegm to create poisonous pearls. Someday you'll have to return her to the sea or hire another wizard to do this same job, over and over again, until her body can no longer endure transmutations.

"Will she die?" I asked, suddenly terrified at the thought of losing my daughter.

"Worse. She'll become what you despise."

"No, that will never happen. I swear. I swear. I'll transmute her body as many times as necessary, but I won't let her turn back into a fish."

I have found a roof over our heads. It's far from what I dreamed of, but it's a good start, especially because no one pays too much attention to Lis. No one finds her amiss despite her hoarse voice, her half-tongue words, and her slovenly steps.

When someone inquires after my daughter's health, I tell them she's recovering from injuries inflicted by the sirens. The scars on her legs and body would vouch for my story.

She doesn't seem to remember anything of the past.

I've fessed up almost everything, Lis. I murdered your mother, sold off your sisters, tortured your body, and made you human. I cheated, stole, and lied. I've earned multiple life sentences, but it was worth it. For your sake, everything would be worth it.

You grew up as happily as you could be in the midst of dirt and dung. My desire to give you a better house, a place to dream, never came to fruition. My credits weren't enough, Lis. Less than five years after your first transmutation, I discovered a scale on you while I was bathing you. I panicked. Fear. I was going to lose you. Soon you'd start to sprout gills, stop talking, and gasp for air. The damned tail that made you the enemy of my species would emerge again.

That night, Lis, I grabbed our last credits. They barely covered your new reconstruction process. All the savings of a life on the high seas were depleted, eaten away, in order to give you a few more years of humanity.

The wizard received us again with a cynical smile on his face. Still, he rebuilt your bones, prevented your tail from growing, and transmuted your scales and gills. You were normal again, Lis, despite the pain from your treatments, the stitches *(sting like needles, Papa)* pricking your feet when you took a step, and the choking fits that violently assaulted you night after night.

I knew then as I do now that this would haunt us for the rest of our lives. Five or six more years with you, and then what? Murder you? See how you became a fish, my daughter, capable of spitting poisonous pearls and causing waves that would swallow towns, villages, and people?

I wanted to save my money, Lis. I grew old and turned into a wretch who counted breadcrumbs and reduced expenses to a minimum. I poisoned the rest of your childhood.

I loved you, Lis. I love you, my daughter—so much so that I forsook my tattered honor and joined a tribe of debt collectors. They hired me to torture those who couldn't pay their taxes and tithes to the Yugular tribal chiefs. My shame became shredded, something insignificant like a leprosy-affected hand. I had to get rid of my dead member to continue and earn credits, coins, which would pay for your treatments.

Years passed, Lis. During your second transmutation, you had a suffocation crisis that almost cost you your life. I had to carry you in my arms to the sea and submerge your body. You breathed again under the water.

"Papa, I don't feel well." Your hoarse voice cracked, reminiscent of the shrieks spewed forth from deep within your mother—terror, uncertainty, and the approaching end. "What's wrong with me?"

"Just the aftereffects of an accident, Lis."

Eight months had passed since your third transmutation.

"She won't walk again," said the wizard with his usual smile. "Her bones won't grow anymore."

The pain of your treatments was so bleak, Lis, that one especially terrible night—when your screams threatened to drive me crazy—I thought of the merciful harpoons that would penetrate your adoles-cent body, how you'd thank me for being such a good father.

"It hurts all the time," you confided in me afterward, your eyes brimming with tears. "Papa, I think I'm going to die."

It was your ultimate transformation, Lis. I couldn't avoid it despite so many attempts. The curse of the thorn sails through my veins, remember? Your mother's revenge. All that, all at once.

Two days later, you crawled out of bed. You couldn't speak anymore. Or you didn't want to. Your eyes looked at me for a moment and I knew, Lis, that some spring of rage and memory had shot up inside you. You had your mother's gaze and the sirens' hatred against my kind. Then you spit white saliva and wrapped it around your fingers until you made a ball, a magnificent egg. You offered it to me...laden with poison.

You knew everything, Lis. You remembered your childhood as an orphan. Your nature subverted. Your abduction. The sheer misery of occupying a body that didn't belong to you for so many years. The torture and pain I subjected you to with the transmutation. I was your enemy, and the pious harpoon flashed through my mind again. I kept one, just for safety, but I never thought I'd have to use it against you. As you lay on the bed, scales began to spread across your belly and face: you solidified them, Lis. Something in you spoke and told you should do it because I dreamed of killing you.

I didn't kill you, despite your hatred. Your tail began to emerge from where your legs were before. I couldn't bring myself to go through with it, even though your gills grew as you gasped for air.

A new phlegm. A new pearl. You extended your hand for a second before you jerked it away.

That night you spewed mist. You thought, no doubt, that I was asleep and thus you'd succeed in killing me. No. You're dumb, Lis. You don't know me at all. Don't you remember I'm a veteran of wars against your kind? I watched over you, my daughter, and I read signs of urgency in you. The mist didn't sneak up on me.

I dashed out of our cramped room, Lis, in search of fresh air. The harpoon was in my hands. I waited outside the labyrinthine building. You were coming out, Lis, crawling over the rubble and dirt. In search of the sea.

Do you want my confession, my daughter? The real curse of the thorn has touched me. You're under my harpoon and you scream with all your siren nature. Hatred flashes in your eyes because I'm your enemy. But my harpoon remains in my hand, death doesn't descend on you, as my hand freezes.

This is the sea, Lis, what I always denied you. The world that exists beyond mine: your world. The waters stained with blood where you'll seek to avenge years of suffering. You'll be cruel. You'll spit mist and poisonous pearls, and you'll forge those waves that wreak havoc on ports across the kingdom. And perhaps, daughter, you'll meet your death in another harpoon, trapped like your mother between a wave and her offspring.

This is the sea, Lis. Leave now and never come back. Don't you ever hope to kill me or make me pay for all the evil deeds I have committed. The curse of the thorn you now hurl at me with your gaze can't be worse than seeing you submerge back to the bottom of the waters.

My harpoon slips out of my hand and falls on the ground.

At my feet lies the last piece of your memories—a round pearl shining like a siren's scale. And from the sea, there in the distance, a blurred mass of darkness hovers.

A swirl of mist encroaches closer and closer toward me.

Liam Hogan

The Peculiarity of Two

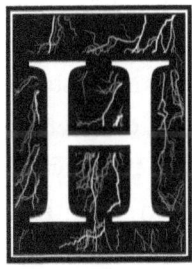

OODED EYES STARE with fierce intensity across the scarred oak table as the creature looms out of the shadows. "I had never thought to see another..." he muses.

I nod my glass of claret in Adam's direction. The dregs glint like drops of spilled blood in the candlelight. "From the moment I became aware, I knew of *your* existence. Knew that we were two of a kind. Knew that this day was destined to come."

As if reassured, he eases back into the gloom, his chair protests the shifting weight. Then the inn once again lapses into silence. The few staff are long gone, there is no-one to clear the tables, to refill our glasses.

We refill our own. It was Adam who unearthed the handful of candles. They are less harsh than gas lamps, more forgiving. His eyes glint in their wavering light.

I wonder: can Adam smile?

Earlier, in a room above the one in which we now sit, beneath bright incandescent mantles surrounded by the sooty halo of their less efficient predecessors, Adam and I compared notes. Compared bodies. Adam knows little of the experiments that brought him to life, that keep him alive unto this day. I have the dubious benefit of a longer relationship with my creator, but there are mysteries still. Mysteries that decades of medical research have done nothing to illume, that no doctor or scientist present today can tackle.

We are forced to conclude we are as much the product of blind luck as of science.

I am the *neater* creation. Benefiting from the unstoppable advance of anatomical knowledge, or merely from improvements made to Adam's earlier prototype? Adam is the stronger; much stronger. A strength not explained merely by his large stature. A strength that matches his hunger.

It is as though his body burns fuel at twice my rate. The no-man's land of table between us is littered with the remains of our meal, barely space to rest my empty glass. Most of the dishes are his.

He is, surprisingly, a vegetarian.

I wonder if his diet is more or less efficient than mine. And if it is truly an ethical choice, as he claims, or some limitation of his reconstructed gut?

It is Adam's coin that paid for our food and drink, and for this condemned inn to be exclusively ours, for one night, at least. Adam shrugged my purse away. Both of us have more money than those who previously owned the hands we count our coins with could have ever dreamt. I do not ask how he came by his.

He drums solid fists on the ancient wood, shaking the scraped-clean dishes. Opens one hand—a hand that has maimed and killed beyond number—and looks at it as if it is a thing he has never before seen.

"What now?" he asks the darkness.

I shrug. I have no answer and am doubtful the question was aimed at me.

He was not an easy man to track down. He does not stay long, in any one city, in any one country. It is easier to tell where he has been than where he is going: the bodies have a tendency to mount up. Mostly, they are no-one anyone would miss. Adam has his own peculiar moral compass, a strong sense of justice that protects the innocent, the weak, the feeble minded.

All the things he is not.

And when I did find him, more by chance than by design, I approached with extreme caution, unsure of the reception I would receive until I had convinced him of who and what I am.

Unsure of my reception even once I had done so.

I find myself still unsure.

When first I sought Adam, I was looking for understanding. A way to live in this changing world. A guide, a mentor, a teacher. Later, as one age gave

way to another, ninety-nine rolling over, with tire-
some inevitability, into nought, the beginning and the
end, I longed for companionship. An equal. One who
does not shy away from what I truly am, one who
understands. And long before our unexpected encounter, a quarter of a century on from my painful
rebirth, my search had turned idle and was fuelled
only by morbid curiosity. Even at the very beginning
of my quest Adam had already lived a long life, his
body having lived even longer. And yet, he and it
seem immune to the ravages of time.

My skin is lined, I wear reading glasses. I grow
old. It is unfair; half my span was over before it even
began. I carry both my years and the years of those
who came before me, and fear it will not be the
youngest parts of me that seal my inescapable fate.

What did Adam's creator do, that mine did not?

It is a question whose answer will surely come too
late for me, if it comes at all. On some not so distant
day Adam will be alone once more.

I wonder how he feels about that.

Though, where there are two, there is a
possibility for many. Two is such a *peculiar* number.
Yesterday, he discovered he is no longer unique. It
can only be a matter of time until there is a third of
our kind, until there are perhaps a multitude.

Outside, in the dark, narrow street, someone
hammers on the boarded doors and windows of our
temporary respite. Adam watches as I flinch. The
sudden clamour brings back unwanted memories,

though it is merely a drunk unwilling or unable to accept the scrawled 'We're Closed' sign.

It is not the first such interruption of the evening. But as the hours advance and the candles burn lower, perhaps it will prove the last.

Adam sits impassive, ready and waiting. I have glimpsed the dagger he wears in his belt, have heard tell of his terrible acts of superhuman strength and of the fearsome speed at which his apparent calmness can turn to fury. For a moment, it is my turn to be reassured. Belatedly, I realise that if our space is indeed invaded, if a mob of angry men burst in here and now with axes and torches, Adam would still be sitting impassive and waiting. Waiting to see what *I* would do.

I fear—I *hope*—he would be disappointed.

We were both born of violence, he and I. Our bodies did not come from those who died of natural causes. Accident, or murder, or the punishment the state metes out to those who fall foul of its ever changing laws. There is always plenty of raw material.

I know that Adam has long sought a companion. I know also that he has attempted to sire them. In this, he has failed, often spectacularly. In any case, I suspect he would have been unimpressed with the results. My progeny have turned out no different from countless millions of humans. His, most likely, would be the same. And he would have to watch them grow old and die.

Perhaps his failure to sire offspring is the key to his longevity. Can you have children, if you live forever? Can you live forever, if you have children?

Of course, Adam may merely be long-lived, not immortal. Methuselah, not a fallen angel. Only time will tell.

Time that I do not have.

There are other differences between us, some good, some bad. For me, for him. Adam does not feel pain. Or not as keenly as any normal man. Whereas my senses are, I am convinced, sharper than most and this most definitely includes pain. Why is pain not considered one of the senses? It has always been a mystery to me. It is no mystery that I avoid it wherever possible.

I am made up of fewer people than Adam. My head comes from a single corpse, the brain transferred extant. There are no surgical scars criss-crossing my face or scalp, except the one that traces the length of my spinal column, beginning at the nape and ending at the coccyx.

In the right conditions—and with the right amount of coin—I pass for human and have often done so. I even fell in love once, and was loved back, unlikely though that sounds. Adam did not fully believe me when first I told him we were kin. Not until I stood before him, naked in the bright gaslight, not until he traced the lines across my body with tremulous fingers.

When it came to my turn, I was more assured. I ran my hands across his ragged torso with a sense of fulfilment. His scars are, of course, much older than mine. In areas, they have thickened, knotted, and there the skin still looks raw. In others, the wounds have faded over the many decades and only my fingertips can tell where one body ends and another begins.

Not all of those jagged edges are due to bluntness of his creator's vision, not all of them are quite so ancient. His flesh is not immune to the weapons of lesser, mortal men. Nor to the injury that he himself has inflicted on it, over the near-century of his tortured existence.

I try to look after my patchwork form with more care. Avoid confrontations that could turn violent. Slip by, a shadow, in the darkness. And yet my borrowed body, unlike his, is fading with the years. The cadavers I am formed from were not yet born when those that made Adam started their second life, and yet my hair is gray and worn short, where his is a surprisingly glossy rope of jet black, even if it grows from only one side of his mighty skull. It is an odd vanity, for one so crudely shaped.

In intellect, we have perhaps similar abilities, but unlike Adam, I retain vestigial memories from my former life. I learnt my second language, French, faster than my first, and subsequent research identified the Parisian pickpocket whose head and tongue I own. I sometimes doubt all of the thoughts that inhabit my skull are truly mine.

Adam has been around longer than I. He has had time to learn languages from every continent, though he retains a slight Germanic accent speaking all of them. He has studied more subjects, knows more facts, experienced more events, than I, than anyone. Given the opportunity, which would require circumstances I cannot foresee, Adam could hold his own in discourse against any man, in any society. A keen mind coupled to the accumulated knowledge of a more than average lifespan.

Much of what he has learned, I am sure, he has long since forgotten. Much of it is no longer relevant. Theories ludicrous to the modern mind, proven incorrect by recent experiments. Such is progress. No doubt Adam will live long enough to see their replacements debunked as well.

I think I am a disappointment to Adam. Too unlike him, for all that we both count among the reborn. I am less than the sum of my parts, he, somehow, is more. His strength, his durability, his longevity, suggest that in putting him back together, he someone became *better* than human. As if science can improve on nature. As if the god neither of us believe in could be so easily bested.

I have other faults. I am too talkative, where he is a man of few words. Our conversation stutters and stalls like a carriage propelled by two uneven engines.

At first, we talked of the changes he has seen. The changes we have both seen! The marvels, the impossible feats. Men taking to the air in flimsy constructions of wood and stretched canvas. Loco-motives hurtling across the country, leaping rivers and burrowing through mountains. The discovery of a new planet, and of a dozen new moons. Gaslight replacing candles and, in streets and theatres and surely one day even buildings such as this, electric replacing gas. Already, messages crackle at the speed of thought across the Atlantic, via thick ropes of underwater cables.

And if all of this was not fantastical enough, the dreams of mortal men play across silver screens in temples of futurity.

But what good has any of it done for mankind? Cities bulge at the seams with their new workforces, enslaved to the machine. The air they breathe grows dark, laden with soot. Flames lick at the faces and souls of the desperate. Hovels reek of disease and decay…

Perhaps that is too bleak. Perhaps we are through the worst of it, even as the slums that surround our meeting place are ripped down and rebuilt anew, and doctors refine their understanding of the microscopic life that causes illness. But mankind revels in finding new ways to destroy itself and will do so again. The bright lights of science are turned to weapons, for a war that feels as inevitable as winter.

Perhaps this too will cleanse. Perhaps it will merely destroy. Neither Adam nor I profess to care. It is, after all, not *our* battle. I will do what I can to avoid the coming conflict, and would encourage Adam to do the same, though he refuses to be drawn on the subject. Neither of our bodies are immune to bullets and bayonets and worse. Could that be what he seeks?

Perhaps he will head into the heart of the coming storm and find death and destruction enough for him there.

Not I. Even this island nation no longer feels safe, and an outsider is never safe in times of trouble. And we two monsters will always be outsiders.

The room and the conversation have grown cold and stale. We sit in silence, lost more in the contemplation of our own existence than in each other. For all that we have said, there are volumes unspoken. Perhaps unthought. Tiredness creeps up on us both. Time to go.

In the darkened alley at the back of the pub we clasp hands one last time. For the briefest moment, Adam *squeezes*. It is a vice that brooks no resistance and I feel the bones of my hand grate as pain lances up my arm. I glimpse a glimmer of his wreckage of teeth —a smile—and fear for my life.

Abruptly, he releases me and I watch him vanish into the smog as I catch my breath. Dawn is not far off. I do not tarry.

We shall not meet again, at least, not in so public an arena. Stood beside Adam's, my own peculiarities are thrown into sharper relief. And two monsters are far scarier than one. News of this encounter will spread and people will rightly be afraid. Next time, they might be prepared, might be ready. We are all monsters, when scared.

And so we two reborn go our separate ways. I, to find a new reason to go on. Though in truth this particular quest has not been at the forefront of my mind for a long while and our supposedly predestined meeting having now happened I find it answers no questions, leaves me no better and no worse off than I was yesterday.

And Adam? Wherever he goes, whether towards war or away from it, I suspect he will be paying close attention—to me. I imagine him reading a foreign newspaper, an account of my demise, the strange body I leave behind enough to merit a photograph. I see him a few months later, shirt fluttering in an icy wind, silent before my final resting place, an unmarked grave in unconsecrated ground.

Or perhaps I, or rather my mismatched bones, will end up against my wishes in some eminent anatomist's private collection, as did those of Charles Byrne and Truganina. Or on display in some pathology museum to medical students, like Joseph Merrick. Ghoulish inspiration for a future generation of doctors.

I shiver at the thought and clutch my coat closer.

It is only a week later, when I am on the deck of a passenger ship bound for the Americas with the same coat once again wrapped tight around my all too mortal form, that I realise neither of us mentioned the names of our long dead creators.

Diana A. Hart

A Dog's Death

 **IRENS BATTERED MY EARS.** Osip and I
dashed through the long-dead hamlet,
breath ragged and explosives bounc-
ing against our backs. Subzero air hit
my lungs like a knife. Still I ran, wind
tearing at my stolen uniform, howling as though
Russia herself sought to drive the Wehrmacht from
her borders. My pulse pounded in time with Her
rage. Sang to avenge country and comrade. Spotlights
raked after us, turning frost-slicked walls and razor
wire into a blinding labyrinth.

I ducked into an alley to avoid the lights. "Monastery's this way," I yelled over the klaxons, following
childhood memories towards the village square. In the

distance a Raupenschlepper truck rumbled to life, but it was the Death Dogs that worried me. A low growl echoed between snow-covered cottages, closing fast.

"Stepan, on your left!" Osip shouted.

A monstrosity of fur and stitches burst from a side-street. I yelped and dove aside. The bull-sized brute collided with a house, cracking whitewash and caving bricks inward. Sulfur and dog-reek choked the alley. I brought my Mauser rifle up but the gray, humanoid hound leapt from the rubble before I could draw a bead. I ducked beneath a swipe. Claws gouged brick, peppering my neck with chips. I pulled a knife. The Dog was faster, catching me with a backhand.

Stars popped across my eyes. For a heartbeat I flew. The next I hit cobble. My pack absorbed most of the impact, plastique deforming as it knocked the wind from me, but I still tumbled out of the alley and across the courtyard-turned-motor-pool. My shoulder clipped stone. Fire shot through my collarbone.

"*Suka,*" I wheezed, rolling over and blinking the dots from my vision.

My blood curdled. I'd tumbled more than five car lengths into the open, my Mauser was just out of reach, and the Dog lumbered towards me like a chimp from the Stalingrad zoo. Osip dashed between Opel Blitz trucks, Luger cracking as he fired into the Dog's back. The beast just flicked an ear and kept coming.

My stomach knotted. *Too much muscle!* Osip couldn't kill it from behind. I slid across the cobbles, grabbed my Mauser, and rolled into a firing position.

The Dog snarled. Broke into a run. Silver fur rippled in my sights but I aimed for a chest-suture. Human hair sprouted between the stitches, hinting at the men within the monstrosity. Bile filled my throat.

My rifle boomed. The beast collapsed, but instead of death throes and a crimson flood it just curled tight, gasping in short, foggy breaths. I swore and chambered another round. *Still breathing, still dangerous.* Germans shouted. Blazing searchlights angled toward the courtyard. Osip dove in, cursing, and hauled me to my feet. We rushed behind an Opel, spotlights nipping at our heels.

I rested my back against the high-walled truck-bed, breathing hard as I listened for growls or the inhuman mutterings of more Death Dogs. Osip fell in beside me, sweat beading across his brow, but he didn't press against the truck. I couldn't blame him. Even frozen, the smell of the dead hung in the air, thick enough to taste. Little wonder. Our fellow countrymen were stacked like cordwood in the bed, awaiting their turn in the vats.

My chest lurched. I knew the Wehrmacht were carting the dead out of Stalingrad to make more Death Dogs, but this? Four more trucks sat in the square, each filled to bursting. I shuddered. If we didn't take out the lab now then the liberation of Stalingrad would fail, Zukov's tanks overrun by waves of slathering man-beasts.

"*Dermo,*" Osip gasped and dropped into a crouch. He took a few quick breaths between his knees. "So much for sneaking in."

I shrugged, igniting fresh pain in my shoulder. "It was worth a try."

Equipped with stolen uniforms and guns, our fair-haired team spoke enough German to pass for Nazis. Still, we must have smelled like Russians because the Dogs bayed an alarm once we'd crossed the wall. Between sirens, spotlights, and roving Death Dogs we'd lost track of Pyotr and Gavriil, but Osip and I still had enough explosives to take out the lab. My back tightened. *Probably.*

I shook my head. Gritted my teeth and pressed my fingers against my clavicle. Fresh pain burned, but it was more embers than flame. A wan smile teased my lips. *Nothing broken.* I'd live long enough to push the detonator.

Hoarse, coughing barks rolled across the court-yard. Bare feet slapped cobble. I took a sharp breath, knuckles whitening around my Mauser, and peeked over the hood of our truck. Lanterns bobbed in the distance, whistles blaring as the Wehrmacht pounded towards the market square. Ahead of the throng, swift shadows darted between empty cottages. Broken Russian spilled from dark alleys.

"Catch…Catchcatchcatch," a black-and-tan Dog wheezed during the pass of a spotlight. It shook its head as though clearing away flies. "Kill and catch."

I scowled. The first Death Dog I saw chattered, too. The cream-coated creature had been hunched in Stalingrad's tank assembly, muttering to itself as it gulped down my comrades in wet, red hunks…I huffed and focused on the present. Centered the black-and-tan in my crosshairs.

"Mudak." I squeezed off a round as the Dog flitted between a stack of bodies. A sharp yip told me I'd found flesh. Osip fired around the truck's bumper while I reloaded and scanned the buildings for a bolt-hole that wouldn't scuttle our mission.

My jaw tightened as I took in peeling paint and defaced statues. The Germans had added onto the older structures, turning the peaceful streets of my youth into bunkers and brick corridors, but enough remained for me to get my bearings. Sure enough, I spotted the church's old onion dome to the east, towering above the fortifications like a beacon.

"Osip!" I yelled over the sirens. He glanced at me, breath fogging and eyes wide as a cornered lamb. I flicked my chin towards a pair of double doors. "Through there!" Old monastery brickwork peeked through the frost. As long as the Germans hadn't walled off anything it should be a straight shot for the sanctuary and the atrocities within.

Streaking from cover, a brown Dog ripped the spare tire off one of the Opels and flung it at us. We ducked but the collision still rocked the truck. Frozen bodies tumbled out, clattering against the ground like mannequins.

A distant boom shook the camp, tremors spreading up through my soles. One of the sirens cut out as plumes of hellfire lapped the sky. For a second I could only gape, soaking in the flame. "Pyotr…" Spotlights swiveled towards the blaze, plunging the courtyard into sudden twilight.

I shook my head. Slapped Osip on the shoulder. "Go! Now!"

He fired a few blind rounds, catching the brown Dog in the throat, and dashed for the entry. I backed up after him, firing on Death Dogs as they emerged from the shadows. Firelight edged their hackles in embers and their eyes flashed orange as they moved. Sweat slicked my palms. I dropped two but the rest closed fast, chittering in broken Russian as they leapt effortlessly over trucks and corpses.

"Covering fire!" Osip shouted. I broke and ran for the entryway.

Claws scraped behind me. Rancid breath poured down my collar, spiking my pulse. Osip leaned around the heavy doors and emptied his clip. A half-yelp, half-curse raked my ear. My heart spasmed but the heavy thump and tumble behind me told me that Dog, at least, was down.

I dove through the entry and put my back to the door, helping Osip force it shut and jerk wrought-iron bolts into place. A Dog slammed into the wood, bending the locking mechanism. We pushed back. Barely dropped the crossbar into place before the others rammed the doors.

Wood groaned but held. Sweat dripped from my brow. Pale as a turnip, Osip fumbled twice as he reloaded. Dogs whimpered and tore at the doorframe. The black-and-tan I'd shot pressed his bloody muzzle to the gap, sniffing deeply. Plaintive moans slipped through the wood.

"Little hares. Crunchy hares. Crunchcrunch-crunch." Gibberish devolved into laughter.

Skin crawling, I grabbed Osip's elbow and pushed him down the plaster hall. Dim bulbs lined the corridor and exposed cords spoke of hasty installation. Animal urine stung my nose. Iron gates walled off what used to be priests' quarters, and the residents —everyday hounds, incapable of speech and standing on all fours—peered between the bars. Some bared their teeth and barked at us while others bristled at the wooden doors, flinching with every impact.

As we passed the kennels Osip's brow knit. "Poor pups. I didn't know they were still alive when, well..."

I laughed, low and bitter. "Save your pity. They're all monsters."

A live canine formed the core of every Death Dog, muddled together with blood and bone of our fallen, until all that remained was one of those things pounding at the door. Acid gnawed my gut. By the Motherland, I'd destroy the kennels, too, but without Pyotr and Gavriil we could barely bring down the lab.

"You know why the Wehrmacht use dogs for the base, don't you?" I growled. Osip just hurried down the corridor. I jogged after, seething. "Only a dog can love a Nazi."

Heading for the church's nave, Osip turned down a statue-lined hallway. I toppled a stack of crates in our wake. Wood snapped and disgorged tins of meat, choking the corridor. Combined with the low ceiling the mess should slow any pursuit.

Osip reached the nave entrance before me. He pressed his back to the wall and reached across the doors, testing the handle. His nose wrinkled.

"It's barred."

A low, electronic hum emanated from the church. A quick glance behind confirmed we were alone. *But it won't stay that way.* Outside sirens still droned, whistles chirped, and the pounding on the doors gained a creaking, splintering quality. My mouth went dry. I pulled my pack around, wincing as the strap rubbed my injury, and dug out a shaped charge.

Osip sucked in a breath. He relocated behind a statue of St. Boris while I slapped the ball of PVV-5A on the door. Counting seconds, I ducked behind St. Gleb's stone robes.

The explosion rattled my bones. Brick, plaster, and bits of wood battered the statue. Stray chips sandpapered my skin. Half the ceiling collapsed and glacial air poured into the hall, thinning the dust and smoke. Through the haze I glimpsed gargantuan vats filled with radiant, yellow-green fluid. Flayed dogs bobbed in the cylinders, suspended by a nest of tubes and wires, twitching as though chasing rabbits in their sleep.

Six riflemen rushed in front of the stasis tubes, leveling Mausers. *"Schiessen!"* one barked.

Bullets hissed past, pocking walls and showering us with plaster. Osip and I pressed tighter against the statues. Adrenaline coursed through my veins. Bubbled up as laughter. "From fire to flame, yeah?" I yelled over the crack of gunfire.

"Yeah." Osip dug out his own ball of plastique, shifting wires in the mass. "Life's no meadow." A stray shot shattered St. Boris' fingers. Osip flinched but kept working.

I swapped my rifle for my Luger. Done tinkering, Osip flicked a small salute. I leaned around my statue and fired at the stasis tubes. Glass burst. Waves of yellow-green fluid crashed through the church, engulfing several Wehrmacht and pouring ankle-deep through the ruined doorway. Rotten-egg-stink burned my nostrils. Osip stepped out of cover and hurled his plastique. Red burst from his thigh. He fell, cursing. Another explosion rocked the church.

Foul clouds roared from the nave, clogging my throat with a rotten, chemical taste. I doubled over coughing. My heart raced, expecting gunfire and German shouts, but only the patter of rock and a guttering whine of damaged machinery echoed from the sanctuary.

"*Chert voz'mi!*" Osip cursed. He clamped one hand against his thigh. Used the other to pull himself to a pile of collapsed brick. I rushed over, vat-broth splashing underfoot, and helped him into a sitting position. His weight made my shoulder scream.

I scowled at his wound. Mangled flesh yawned beneath ruined fabric. "Non-lethal?"

"Yes." He tore a strip from his uniform and cinched it over the injury, hissing between his teeth. Blood slowly colored the fabric. "For long enough, anyway."

Splintering wood echoed from the kennels. I stiffened. *Please, just another minute.* Osip gestured for me to help him up. I hauled him to his feet, threw his arm over my good shoulder, and shuffled around the rubble. Acrid fluid soaked through my uniform. "I'll set the packs. Just keep them off me, yeah?"

Osip tipped his weapon. "Yeah."

Still, worry chilled me as we hobbled into the sanctum. Once the long, arched room had filled me with awe, gold leaf and painted saints inspiring dreams of peace. Now all that remained were chipped frescos and the reek of sulfur. Far to my right, the foyer doors were barred from the inside and lavishly carved staticidia had been replaced with rows of gurneys. I glanced left, past the altar to the templon, searching the gilded wall for the Beautiful Gates and the room beyond. I found only more vats, bodies in various states of dissection, and a scorched scientist slumped over a half-finished Dog. Bellows forced air in and out of the vivisected creature.

Anger boiled through me. So many of my brothers died the same way in Stalingrad, honorable men bleeding out over half-finished tanks until the Volga ran red as an open vein. I spat at the scientist's corpse as we passed. Once we destroyed this place the Germans would run out of Dogs, Zukov would retake Stalingrad, and the Wehrmacht would be left to fatten crows.

"Here's good," Osip said, slipping free of my

shoulder. He limped to a pile of rubble across from our ragged entrance, debris granting cover and good sightlines of both hall and foyer. Osip settled into a sniper's crouch. The shadow of a chandelier encircled him, as though the church sought to shield them.

I swallowed. "Osip, I—"

Gibbering wails echoed from the hall. "Crunchy hares?"

"Make it fast, Stepan." Osip's voice trembled.

I tossed him a Mauser and ammo from a dead soldier. "Quick as a sparrow."

While Osip kept his gun trained on the hall, I dragged his explosives towards an armored generator and drums of fuel. I dropped the pack and armed the remote detonator.

Osip's gun boomed. An inhuman screech stabbed my ears. "Three in the hall!"

"More time!" I spun in a quick circle, trying to decide where to plant the second pack. The vats were tempting, but if I collapsed a support I could bring the whole roof down on us.

Osip fired again. Pained yelps devolved to growls. Stone snapped and St. Gleb's torso flew out of the hall, crashing down centimeters from Osip's head.

I froze. The hall had a clear view of the vats. And judging by that throw, I was well within range. *Pillar it is.* Pulse fast, I squeezed between the gurneys for a central support.

I passed a young woman—couldn't be more than nineteen—split open on an operating table, lifeless eyes boring into mine. My stomach bucked. Brown hair littered the slab. Her shaved skull hung open and empty. Freckled skin had been pinned back, exposing bone and what was left of her viscera. Large spindles held her muscle fiber, wound up like yarn and submerged in pans of that same yellow-green fluid.

I tasted bile. Battlefield gore was one thing, but this—

The templon moved, Beautiful Gates swinging open. Moonlight caught an SS uniform.

"Fass!" the officer shouted.

Adrenaline arced through me. I raised my Luger, expecting a Death Dog, but a mere Doberman streaked past him. I gasped and corrected my aim. Bullets ping-ed off gurneys and marble façade, missing the blur that raced towards me. "No!" The maze of corpses kept me from backing up. *"Dermo, derm—"*

The Doberman leapt for my gun. Fangs dug deep into my flesh, wrenching me towards the ground. My heavy pack did the rest. I fell. Hard. The detonator skittered off under a gurney.

My heart thundered. The Doberman whipped his head back and forth, savaging my arm and keeping me off balance. Pain roared through me. I reached under the gurney for the detonator. All I found was soaked tile. Blind panic took over. I screamed, beating the dog with my fist.

Osip's shouts cut through my own. I caught glimpses of him between the Doberman's kill-shakes. A black Death Dog bounded over the rubble.

Wrapped its hands around Osip's throat, howling as it pounded him against the floor. The injured black-and-tan bounced from foot to foot nearby, sobbing and muttering about hares.

Boots clacked against tile. The SS officer strode into the nave, blonde hair deathly pale in the moonlight. He pointed at Osip. *"Aus."* His German was crisp as his uniform. "I want them alive." The black Dog froze, Osip slack in its grip. The officer's hawkish features pinched. *"Aus!"* Ears flattening, the monster tossed Osip onto the rubble and backed away.

I stayed perfectly still, jaw locked and hardly breathing as the Doberman growled around my arm. As long as I didn't move the mutt seemed content to grind its teeth into my flesh instead of tossing me about like a rag doll. Sweat rolled down my back. I inched my fingers further under the gurney.

"Ritter," the officer called. The Doberman's stumpy tail wriggled. His master pointed at the detonator. *"Bring."*

Teeth pulled free with a soft sucking noise. I made a grab for the detonator but Ritter was faster. My chest lurched as he snapped up the device, taking any hope I had of completing my mission with it, and trotted to the officer's side.

"Sitz." Ritter dropped to his haunches, snorting around the trigger. A quick pat made the dog vibrate with excitement. The officer plucked my Luger from the floor and crouched over me. With both Ritter and Death Dogs at his command, all I could do was scoot

back, trembling.

"You," he said in butchered Russian. "There will be questions."

He struck my temple. Blackness claimed me.

~~~

Hell dug beneath my fingernail, forceps scraping keratin as the scientist angled for a better grip. Raw meat burned where my other nails should be. I gritted my teeth, traced every crack and chip in the bare walls, even chanted songs in my head to escape the pain. A tall order.

My head throbbed, cuts and burns dappled my naked body, and the air was cold enough to make my breath plume.

The SS officer watched it all. He stood across from me, posture stiff and expression dark, only breaking composure to reach down and massage Ritter's ear. The Doberman groaned and leaned into the touch. A surgeon in gore-stained scrubs ticked off his fingers as he delivered a report.

"...multiple spine fractures, punctured lung, and probable concussion. Even if the Red wakes up he won't feel torture, much less survive it." He nodded towards me. I kept my face blank, trying to hide I could comprehend German. "That one's all you have, Major."

Frigid air turned suffocating. Osip. I'd failed him. Failed Stalingrad and Mother Russia. I balled my free hand, ruined fingertips burning. *No. Just wait for an opening…* If I got loose I could still light off those fuel drums, maybe disable the generator. Provided I could get past the Death Dog…The tricolor brute stood in the doorway, expression a dazed mass of sutures, hackles twitching with every clink of surgical tools.

Forceps clicked as they locked in place. Exhausted, I barely shuddered. My torturer glanced over his shoulder.

"Major Bernau?"

The officer lifted his chin. "Again, sabaka," he said in Russian. "You from Stalingrad? Tanks coming?"

Discipline and a dash of delirium held my tongue. I closed my eyes and hummed 'The Cossack's Parable' in my head. *Ah, it's not yet evening, it's not yet evening…* Memories stirred like ghosts: singing with my comrades as we welded tank armor, drinking along the Volga river, even our breath freezing in our beards as we hiked through Stalingrad.

The scientist pulled my nail. I yowled, twisting against my restraints. A word from Bernau cut the torment short. I fell back, panting.

"Is Zukov coming?" Bernau watched me as a falcon does a mouse. "How many troops?"

A weak laugh slipped out. "I've scarcely…had… any sleep," I sang softly. Each word was like lifting lead with my tongue. Still, I kept going, the Cossack's Parable soothing me sure as sip of vodka. "And oh I've dreamed of what's to come."

The corners of Bernau's eyes pinched. He nodded. Forceps twisted. There was a soft pop and white-hot-hell exploded across my senses. I howled, body arched, as the scientist scrambled back in surprise. My nail hung from his forceps, red and rimmed with flesh.

"Major, I'm sorry, I—"

"An abattoir would yield finer work," Bernau sighed, plucking the forceps from his hand. The Major paced to a metal cart—Ritter following at perfect heel —and dropped the implement into a tray of surgical tools. By the door, the Death Dog flinched.

A few ragged breaths, heavy with sulfur and the scent of old meat, chased the blobs from my vision. Blood flowed warm down my hand, pat-pat-patting against the floor. The tricolor Dog stared and licked its chops. Bile stung my throat. I gulped and looked away. Hummed in my head again. *In the dream that came to me, my raven-black horse was raging, dancing, gamboling beneath me.*

The surgeon crossed his arms. "As we told you, Major, we're men of science, not torturers. High Command will have an interrogator here in two days."

My gut knotted. *Two days?* It would be a week before reinforcements reached Stalingrad, T-34s rolling down the Volga in a wall of steel and vengeance. If I broke before then the Wehrmacht would have time to fortify, even deploy enough Death Dogs to hold the city until General Winter starved my comrades into retreat. My jaw clenched. I had to hold on. Find a way to get loose and light off those drums.

Doubt crept in like frost. "Ah, and evil winds came up out of the east," I sang, chasing it back. The

Dog in the doorway cocked its head, eyes brightening amongst the web of sutures as I grew louder. "And they ripped the black cap from that wild head of mine!"

Bernau just clicked his tongue and turned to the scientists. "We cannot wait. The Reds are advancing, and we play a part in their strategy." He let out a long sigh. "What about live splicing?"

Pain, exertion, and the lump on my head left my senses swimming. I dangled my chin to my chest and hummed a few bars while the Wehrmacht sheep bickered about what to do with me.

"There's predicting which personality will be dominant, Bernau. The risks—"

"Are greater if we do nothing." He stroked Ritter's head, caressing the animal with a slow somberness. "And you said yourself there are ways to weight the emergence."

A gravelly hum, off-key but in time, joined mine. I lifted heavy eyelids. The Death Dog straightened up, chin high and shoulders square, proud breaths straining the stitches on its chest. My throat tightened. *It can't be.* Intellect flickered in mangled features. Pulse fast, I spoke the next lines of The Cossack's Parable:

"And the captain was a clever one, he was able to decipher my dream."

The conversation died. I barely noticed, Wehrmacht slipping away along with my pain, the tang of blood, and everything else as I watched the Dog's jaw tremble. Clawed hands curled and uncurled. The beast gulped.

"Ah…i-it will cooome off…"

My heart lurched. *They're still in there!*

"No! Stop! *Pfui!*" the surgeon shouted, arms waving as he hurried for the Dog. The scientist dashed after.

I heaved against my restraints, shouting over them as tears burned down my cheeks, trying to draw out whatever was left of my comrades. "It will come off, he said, that wild head of yours!" Scientist and surgeon tried to scruff the Dog, but it tossed its head and flailed, slapping them to the ground as its craggy voice boomed in time with mine. "Ah, it's not yet evening, it's not yet eve—"

"*Gib laut!*" Bernau snapped.

Ritter let out a thunderous bark. The tricolor brute flinched. Snarling and snapping, Ritter backed the Death Dog into a corner, pounding my ears and draining the light from the creature's expression.

"No! It's not yet evening, and I've scarcely had any sleep!" Screaming seared my throat but I couldn't let my comrades die again, turn back into a dumb, brute beast. The chair groaned as I pulled against my restraints. "Come on, brother! I've scarcely had any sleep, and oh, I've dreamed of what's to come!"

The Death Dog slumped like snow in summer, melting beneath Ritter's abuse. Its voice died to a gravelly whine. Bernau strode up to the creature, spine straight and hands clasped behind his back. Only the faint tremble of fingertips betrayed his unease. He lifted his chin and glowered at the Dog.

"Achtung."

A jolt went through the creature. Its brow smoothed, as much as stitches allowed, and the man-bright shine faded from its eyes. Bernau smiled. The Dog just stood there, breath fogging.

"Fuss."

Ritter settled to Bernau's left, stumpy tail flying. The Death Dog plodded to the right.

Tears blurred my eyes. "In the dream that came to me," I called, watching for an ear-flick, tail twitch, anything...The beast sat. Bernau patted it on the shoulder. Ruffled its ears. I drew a ragged breath, voice little more than a whisper. "My raven-black horse was raging, dancing, gamboling beneath me..."

Bernau praised them both. Ritter wiggled as best he could without stepping out of place. The Dog broke into a dull, happy pant. The surgeon and the scientist picked themselves off the floor, cautious as rabbits.

"Prep the Red. I've some reeducation to see to," Bernau said.

With that he was gone, headings into the hall with both creatures in tow. I slumped in my chair, heart so empty I barely noticed the chill on my skin or the sour taste on my tongue. Motherland forgive me, I barely fought when the surgeon put a needle in my arm and filled my blood with something that made the world spin.

ιιιι

Consciousness eluded me like fish beneath the

ice, the world little more than quiet, unreachable shadows sliding past before I even knew they were there. I groaned and curled tighter. Part of me yearned to stay adrift, to slumber in these dark, numbing waters, but a heart-sore twinge pushed me towards the surface. I sucked down a breath.

Home. That was the first sensation that washed over me. A blanket rested across my shoulders and my lumpy, overstuffed bed cradled my aching bones. Familiar scents soothed like balm: hair and straw from my bed, old marrow bones, and still-fresh hints of Bernau.

My nose wrinkled. *Bernau?*

I jolted into a sit. Pain sliced across by body, wildfire tracing my limbs and muscle. Light poured into unready eyes. I yelped and threw up an arm, blinking fast to clear the glare. My pulse quickened. Seconds ticked by but my vision failed to improve, leaving me in a swimming, fishbowl-like haze. Then I spotted the sutures. Great lines of them criss-crossed my skin.

I jerked back, bruising my spine against the wall. Black-and-tan fur covered my arms, my hands, everything...Ice filled my gut. Dark nails sprouted from where ruined fingertips should be. And my nose! A broad, furry wedge stretched from my face, nose pad drying as I pulled in panic-fast breaths.

Blood roared in my ears. Fighting panic, I looked down.

A horror of wrong angles, twisted muscle, and

sleek fur greeted me, held together by a web of sutures. Tremors wracked my body. Made my fur stand on end. "It's not...I can't..." My throat ached as the wrong voice spilled from it. Sharp teeth cut my tongue.

My stomach bucked. I pitched off the bed, planting not-quite hands to catch myself, as spasms forced yellow-green fluid out. Rotten egg-tasting mess splashed across tile. Lurch after lurch hit me, pushing up liters of fluid and with it any hope this was a hallucination, some fevered dream brought on by whatever they'd dosed me with. The taste was too bitter. The scents too strong, incisions too hot. A final retch dribbled the last of my stomach contents across the floor. I collapsed on my side, whimpering.

This was real.

Breath ragged, I tried to calm down. Little use. My mind tossed like a raging steed, adjusting to my new reality and the wild, untamed senses that flooded my consciousness. Heaven help me, there were so many sounds: the distant whine of machinery, sloshing plumbing, tromping boots, and muffled conversations, even a mouse gnawing the bookshelves lining the room...A bevy of smells assaulted me, too, but it was the mix of sweat, aftershave, and a tiny hint of liver treats that my brain kept zeroing in on. *Bernau.* A happy, warm-gold haze spread through my skull.

Spiders crawled across my skin. *I'm wrong in the head, too.* I growled and tottered to my feet, graceful as a newborn foal. I have to get out of here! Tilting my muzzle just the right way, I found could force my

vision into a crude clarity. I searched the alien surroundings for a door, a window, anything.

A quick sweep revealed furnishings I'd never seen,
yet they filled me with an old, familiar comfort.
Bookshelves and a large, scribbled paper covered the
wall closest to the machine-whine. More shelves and
Bernau's lavish oak desk sat opposite, backed by a
crackling hearth and a shaded floor lamp. A phonograph waited next to the door and, judging by the
particular smell of vinyl, Bernau had loaded his favorite record. Drool pooled across my tongue. That
album meant dinner was coming.

My pulse skipped. Screamed against the traitorous
fog in my skull. I clung to my hatred, my pain, and
shook my head. Shouted and pounded the wall until
my knuckles bled. "This isn't home!" The words
came out a garbled, growling mess. Still, my agony
was enough that the dumb, happy haze retreated.

As my faculties returned the paper on the wall
took on new meaning. My ears flattened. I paced
closer, tracing the widening blue line with a claw. *It's
the Volga...* Pins and tiny flags marked recent battles,
some of which I recognized. A note hung next to a
hamlet outside Stalingrad, restrained German print
listing a date and 'four Reds; two captured.'

My thoughts cleared like I'd taken a dip in the
river. I had to stop Death Dog production! If I didn't,
the liberation of Stalingrad would fail. My pulse
quickened. *There's still time!* If Zukov had already
attacked, Bernau would've disposed of me.

I staggered for the exit. Claws clicked against tile, reminding me that even if I succeeded, the Wehrmacht had still turned me into a monster. My muzzle wrinkled. When this was done I'd kill Bernau, but for now he'd made a grave mistake. In this new body I could walk straight up to the generator, break open the drums, and burn the place down before the Wehrmacht figured out anything was amiss. I reached for the door, growling. *And if they try to stop me, well—*

The knob turned on its own. I jumped back. Grabbed the corner of the desk to keep from falling. Bernau stopped in the threshold, brandy under one arm and clutching a plate of mett and liverwurst. He kept his eyes from widening but I heard his pulse accelerate. I balled my fists. That strange warmth bubbled up again, holding me back. Bernau flashed a smile and came inside. Nudged the door shut. Stress-sweat tinged the air.

"Hungry, Ritter?" he said, starting the phonograph.

The name lanced through my brain, driven deeper by the symphony that burst from the record player. Warm-gold idiocy bounded to the surface. My jaw lolled open and a happy wriggle traveled down my back, setting my stumpy tail flying.

"No!" I yelled in Russian. I clawed at the stitches covering my skull. Swayed on my odd-angled legs and roared over the music. The haze pressed down on me, warning I'd get a swat to the rear if I kept barking, but I pushed back with images of Osip limp and bleeding, of my brothers sprawled shot and half-eaten over their work, even the girl's corpse staring after me with dead eyes. "Stepan!" I howled. The haze weakened but a stitch in my throat popped. Blood coated my tongue. "I am Stepan!"

Bernau cleared his desk and set down his cargo. His breath trembled.

"Ritter. *Fuss.*"

Joyous stupidity engulfed me. A quick scramble ended with a crash on the floor. My elbows stung but I kept going, crawling around the corner of the desk before I regained control, halting arm's reach from Bernau. He watched the whole display from the corner of his eye.

"*Fuss,* Ritter, or no treat."

Moisture welled in his gaze as he spread liverwurst on a cracker. The food snapped. He swore, grabbing the treat before it hit the floor.

I whined between clenched teeth. He was so sad. So scared. I read it in his frown, smelled the adrenaline and tension on him, an almost metallic bite that leached through his uniform. I swallowed. If I just licked his face he'd—

"No!" I snarled and reared onto my hind legs. Bernau looked up at me, not bothering to run, hawkish features softened by loss and a fragile smile. Knots twisted my back. I grabbed him by the shoulders. Every centimeter of me ached to shoot him, to stab him, to tear his head off and crunch-crunch-crunch him between my teeth. But for every act of violence my mind warned of even worse punishments: a stern word, a flick of water across the face, even being put in sit-stay and ignored.

I shook, unable to move as the two drives warred within me.

Slow as snowfall, Bernau reached up and rubbed my ear. My eyes flickered shut. I groaned and leaned in. Some strange, angry corner of my mind howled and dug at me like it was trying to escape a kennel. I ignored it and let my muscles relax.

"Good boy, Ritter."

Bernau's voice caught. I opened my eyes and stuck my nose in his face. He laughed, scratched my chest, then gave me a tiny shove. "Now, *sitz.*"

I plopped down by his ankle. A heart-sore twinge whined in my head. Said sitting with bare balls on the floor was wrong, but I didn't care. The fire warmed my back, Bernau smiled at me, and a liverwurst cracker dangled in front of my nose. I opened my mouth. He plopped the musky meat between my fangs.

While I wolfed down the food and licked crumbs off the floor, Bernau poured himself a shot of brandy and gulped it down. Poured himself a second and whistled. I snapped my head up, ears perked. Bernau waggled a mett-covered cracker.

"You want it, Ritter?"

I shuffled to face him and nudged his knee. Bernau just stared at me. I chuffed. He cocked an eyebrow. That angry little whine started in my head again, feeding off my frustration, so I rolled my shoulders and barked. "Yes."

Bernau let out a relieved chuckle. "Okay then." He took another sip and settled deeper into his chair. I kept my eyes glued to the treat. Bernau's voice turned order-hard. "Tell me: are there troops coming?"

More food and the need for Bernau's approval had me digging though memories faster than a terrier flushing rats. Images of tanks—four packs of ten —rolled down the bank of a river, heading to the city where Bernau's friends stayed. I opened my mouth, but a tiny, heart-sore twinge held me back. My brow wrinkled.

Bernau clicked his tongue. *"Gib laut,* Ritter."

I whimpered. Bernau's expression creased with growing worry. My ears drooped. I couldn't make him sad.

German spilled from my lips like rain.

Jonathan Duckworth

Silvergloom

S THERE *another life? Shall I awake and find all this a dream? There must be, we cannot be created for this sort of suffering.*

As spume rises from the ocean's churn, these words recrudesce to the surface of the consumptive poet's mind. Sickly John has awoken in the small hours, not from any judder or groan or tremor of the ship—the *Maria Crowther* is still as a coin on a pane of glass on these becalmed Portuguese waters—but rather from the protestations of his interior sea, the lifting tides in his lungs that bring the cough. Somehow the others who share the cabin have kept their sleep. The gentle diminuendo of their breathing fills the air—his friend, Joseph, the kindly captain, plump Mrs. Pidgeon, even his fellow consumptive, lovely Miss Cotterell seem immersed in the spell of impenetrable sleep.

Shuddering, sweating from every pore, John abides a time on his berth—just a little coffin-small coffer built into the hull of the ship. He and the others are each cached like a bee in their own comb, but without any of the sweet gold liquor enjoyed by those apian nymphs. How far he feels now from the joy of the daylight hours when he watched whales drifting languidly through the silken blue waters, how far he feels from his poetry, from the vibrant impulse that only weeks ago addressed his bright star in words that sang from the page. How advanced his aching etiolation, his inexorable skid seem.

There's nothing for it. Weak as he is, he feels entombed by the breath of his cabinmates and by the stale dark of the hold, and troubled enough to rise on his feet. He is quiet, first collecting his shoes and then feeling his way to the door. As the door hinge creaks, a voice, that of his friend, Joseph, dreamy, mutters through the dark, "John?" But John does not stop. She is such a small ship, the *Maria Crowther*, that he overhears the sailors' quiet chatter abovedecks. He liked the ship's name when first he heard of her, her wholesome English character, calling to mind a courteous country maid. She is not a passenger ship, this twin-mast brig, but built for freight, chartered to ferry England's finest coal and its most sophomoric poetry to Naples.

Soon he is on the deck, where the cool northerly night breeze—insufficient to fill the sails but enough to grace him—soothes his nerves and aches more than any elixir of mercury could. How it thrills him to think of the long sojourn those winds take from the hollows of brooding Arctic glaciers. Relief is a brief blossoming, as soon the cough shakes him, and the pair of sailors keeping watch midship turn to regard, and then just as soon forget about him, returning to their briar pipes and each other's laconic society. When he looks up, the night sky is like a field of driven snow, only not white but the pale silver of ashes. There is one gap in this field and through it a blot of stelliferous black frames the waxing moon. John follows its rays to the glint on the rail of the ship's bow, and that is when he sees *her*.

For a blink, John imagines it is Miss Cotterell, out for a walk in fresh air like himself, for the figure at the prow has the selfsame litheness and grace as the ailing woman, but he recalls with a shudder that Miss Cotterell is still asleep, and that anyway she could not have come abovedecks without getting by him. There are only two women on the *Maria Crowther*, and both are now in the cabin. Who then does he now see reclining against the rail of the prow?

A long, sinuous appendage gauzed in diaphanous silk beckons to him, and John feels his feet move before he quite makes the decision to approach. But even once he is aware of his own motion he doesn't stop, too curious, too entranced by the shimmer of moon on the woman's naked hair. The sailors watch him pass scarcely with a glance. Why are they untroubled by the woman's presence? They seem not to notice her.

He draws near, and the woman lowers her hand and tilts her head with its pointed, elfin physiognomy, and the silvergloom of the false sun limns the bones of her face and the shape of her eyes and lips, and John feels something like a physical blow to his chest.

"Miss Brawne!" he says, voice cracking as if her presence should devolve him to a stripling's state. It's love, not death that needles him. Were he in the full rose of health, his love would make him ill just the same.

But it isn't Miss Brawne, his bright star, and he knows it almost as soon as he's spoken her name. The woman bears an uncanny resemblance to Fanny Brawne, true, but only if Miss Brawne were drowned and then dredged up after a fortnight pickled in the ocean's brine, and then drowned and recovered again for good measure. Where Fanny's dun tresses would be, instead a damp tack of black kelp ropes from her scalp and coils round her throat. In lieu of blue eyes are a set of milky marbles, pupil and iris alike devoured by cataracts. But it's the woman's teeth that most consume the poet's attention and stoke his awe and terror—twin rows of dark emeralds.

Her breath is the sea's breath. "John Keats. At last you see me."

His words catch in his throat and turn to a violent cough. The pain is brief and hot as a surgeon's spirit flame. When he has recovered, he replies, "You know me, and yet I do not know you, Miss."

"Tut tut," the woman says, and her finger brushes the sleeve of his shirt and through the fabric he feels a chill that pierces to his bone, and a dampness that sods the cloth fast to his skin. "He's a feckless lover to the last who'll not see his bride."

"My—my bride?" John looks to the sailors, and they do not acknowledge him at all this time, their eyes on the ocean.

"In your way you've loved me, and should I not love thee in turn, my Endymion? Or are you lovesick Porphyro? Or are you the gallant knight-at-arms, or perhaps the wretched wight?"

Her voice is playful, girlish. It is Fanny's voice, and yet not.

He steps away, but the woman matches his retreat with a commensurate advance. "Now see here, good woman—" he begins, addressing her as he might a troublesome hawker on a London street.

But she cuts him off, arresting the speech from his throat with a wave of her hand. "No, little poet, let's not bandy in common speech. Where is your lovely poetry for me now? You who called me *now more than ever rich*. Did you know, little poet, that no one has ever called me easeful before you? I watched you as you doted at your brother's sickbed, and even as I breathed him into me, it was you I wanted, you I longed for. Beautiful, sad, vain, precious, guileless poet, you who bled upon the page and you whose name is ever writ in water."

Her brine breath, the clammy air from her skin, the enfolding presence of her shadow, the stench of the ocean's deep slime and old sludge, all of it oppresses him, and he feels incapable of retreat or diversion. He feels himself the sunflower anchored by the tether of the sun's attention, only there is no warmth in her pallid splendor.

He knows he must escape her. He knows, somehow, that to be drawn in nearer, to fall into her embrace, will be a terminal adventure. He wants to call to the sailors for help, but his words fail him, and as he tries to force breath from the flute of his throat, the pain gathers again and he sputters and coughs, ejecting a spatter of blood upon the woman's face.

She does not even blink. "I can stop it, you know. I can deliver you from the twin agonies that circle you like Nimrod's hounds, worrying with their teeth upon your every moment."

He believes her. He knows in fuller measure than he has ever known anything in his brief gasp of a life that she is telling the truth. To fall into splendid dreaming. To sink into the purple draught of the sea. To cast himself into her embrace, accept her touch and be translated from all waking pain to an Ophelian serenity, to the anonymous property and numbing vintage of the deep.

And now she holds a hand to him. "An Italian winter will not save you. You know this, you have seen too much, learned too much from your anatomists' books and the unhappy tack of your life. Why prolong our flirtation? Why not swoon to me?"

He holds a living hand to hers, and she does not grasp it but waits for him to lace his fingers through hers. But he hesitates.

And then a voice calls to him from behind. One of the sailors, a Norwegian. "Hey, Londoner."

The sailor taps his briar pipe on the railing and glowers, as if he'd very much prefer not having to leap into the water to rescue a consumptive passenger.

The woman is gone, and John stands athwart the gunnel of the bowdeck. His hands grasp the railing, while one of his feet dangles over the other side. "Oh," he says. Suddenly he is flooded with the all too familiar toxin of embarrassment. He climbs down from the gunnel, his face flushed. "I rather forgot myself there a moment."

It was, he decides, a passing vision. A trick of the night.

The sailors shake their heads and go back to their watch. On the horizon the coming dawn is a tenuous froth of blue.

When John returns to the cabin, the captain is gone, likely having left for the morning watch, Mrs. Pidgeon snores, and poor Joseph is awake, sitting up in his cot.

"Are you quite all right, old fellow?" Joseph whispers.

"The sea is as yet flat," John answers.

As John climbs into his little nook, Miss Cotterell

begins to cough. Her fit is mercifully short, and when it ends, she speaks. "Did you see him too?" she asks.

John doesn't answer, presuming Miss Cotterell is only babbling in her sleep. And yet he's sure he feels her eyes through the dark.

"Did you see him, Mr. Keats?" she whispers. "Oh, he was so lovely. So kind, and he spoke so softly to me."

"I know not of whom she speaks," Joseph says. "We received no visitors."

None, anyway, that a man of health could perceive.

John will see the woman again, standing on the docks of Naples as he endures the stale heat and squalor of a ten-day quarantine in the port. He will see her on the hills of Lazio during the arduous carriage ride to Rome, and he will see her in the eternal city as well, first as the shape that adumbrates the threshold of his little apartment, then as the shadow that flickers over his sickbed as his lungs dissolve, and finally, when all poetry has fled, then at last he accepts her hand—her kiss—with the rapture of a mercy long deferred.

John Adams

The Well-Trained
Thing in Constance's
Dress

EHOLD!" commands Professor Bright-
fever. And because it is Professor Bright-
fever, you behold. Oh, I suppose we
all behold, for we are all behold*en* to
this handsome scoundrel, tethered to
our lives with his compliments and extortions.

But you are beholden most of all, dear Simon. His
"precious pupil." He will break you, my love. Not
merely break your heart, your spirit. He will break
you.

Professor Brightfever points to the peak of the
velvet-lined staircase. There, high above us partygoers,
is the spectacle he assembled for our amazement. His
latest creation. His latest calamity. It hunches over,

facing away, sludgy hair staining its dress.

We all recognize that dress. How could we not? It is Constance's dress. That colossal, pink affair with billows of ruffles and pillows of frills. Remember, Simon? Remember her prancing it around town, knocking over children, suffocating pets, providing herself ample cover whenever she relieved herself in Mrs. Tafferty's shoppe?

No. Of course, you do not remember. Your attentions focused not on wife, but husband.

Professor Brightfever clamps a casual hand on your shoulder, that shoulder you only let me touch in darkness, when your eyes are closed. "The latest scientific miracle!" the professor bellows. "See once again the face of my beloved Constance!"

In response, the figure on the stairs turns. Professor Brightfever is correct. It *does* have his recently departed wife's face.

"But Constance were dead!" shrieks an overjoyed Mrs Tafferty. "Your last explosion at church done 'er in!"

The assembled party-goers bubble in agreement. They coo. They caw. They shush their children. They chide their wives. They threaten to leave their husbands for not being half as brilliant as Professor Brightfever.

Exhibitions like this are a marvel for our tiny town, eager for whatever excitement the professor can conjure. Despite the inherent peril, the townsfolk return, time after time. The farmers dressed in muck-smeared finery. The family-folk pocketing polished flatware. The dignitaries with their sullied dignity. Even my fellow lads from the College of Modern and Unnatural Sciences gleefully titter. (I catch Handsome Pete surreptitiously rubbing that frequently swollen spot in his trousers.)

Professor Brightfever still grips your shoulder, my slender Simon. But we both know his touch never lasts. In the commotion, he pulls from you, casts you aside, eager to elate another random guest.

Your posture wilts.

Predictably.

I look from you to the thing atop the stairs. And I understand. *This* is why you abandoned our cot last night. You helped him.

You stumble away—(whether to be nearer your cherished professor or rid of me, I cannot say)— nearly tripping over your gangly legs as you attempt to cross the crowded hall. Fortunately for your modesty, the crowd's attention remains in steady sway toward the professor's bluster and blaring, his brays and his bays.

"My Constance's face, yes," Professor Brightfever continues, his fingers now fondling another able-bodied student's shoulder. "But not her mind. Not her heart. Not her...body."

The well-trained thing in Constance's dress slowly raises its arms. Rather, it slowly raises what *should* be its arms. Dozens of vine-like tendrils flutter from pink ruffles. Oozing mucous. Barnacled by suckers. Peppered with unblinking eyeballs.

"It's worms!" cries Mrs. Tafferty. "Lady Constance got worms for arms!" She says this not in terror, not in derision, but in delight. Her hands clap-clap-clap, and she leaks tobacco from her decayed grin.

"Not *worms*," you hiss, appalled she would deign such insult on the professor's greatest accomplishment. "They are tentacles, you simple cow." Always his protector.

But Mrs. Tafferty is too enraptured to hear. "Make them worms wear tiny 'ats an' do funny tricks!" The crowd roars. They laugh. They stomp their muddy boots all over the sparkling floors of Brightfever House. (Handsome Pete emits a mid-rub squeak.)

"Come, my dear," Professor Brightfever calls to his creature. "Let us introduce you to new friends."

As the perfectly poised caricature of Constance seeps down the stairs, Professor Brightfever turns back to his guests. "No doubt, your simple minds are shocked. As well they should be! It was heartbreaking to lose Constance, to become a widower again so recently after Agnes, after Greta, after Allisandra and the others."

"My favorite were the one what turned into a punk'n," screams a little boy before his mother scolds him for confusing the professor's wives with Cinderella's stagecoach.

"But by using my knowledge of Modern and Unnatural Sciences," Professor Brightfever continues, "I figured out how to transform my treasured wife into a new state of being."

"That's somethin'!" yells the village's mayoress. "I

ain't even figured out 'ow that tubby donkey got in me kitchen!"

"I was in my College laboratory," Professor Bright-fever explains, "studying the telescopic equipment. I spotted a many-tentacled being, flying through the cosmos, thrice the size of our planet." (Handsome Pete nears crescendo.) "It spoke to me. Though it was light years away, I heard its words clear as you hear mine. It called itself a 'Stardweller.' It promised rewards. Many rewards. 'Let me be your lowly serv-ant,' it commanded. 'Find me a host form. Transmit my unspeakable essence Earthward.'"

Which is why he enlisted you, naïve Simon. Why you dug up Constance Brightfever's muddy grave. Why you assisted our professor in this unholy reani-mation, this interstellar unification with some being beyond mortal understanding. "Oh, Simon," I whisper. "What have you done?"

But you do not answer. You simply quiver eyelashes at Professor Brightfever. Enthralled.

I understand, my love.

He once enthralled me, too.

"Some College lad brought me Constance's body," Professor Brightfever continues—(does he even know your name?)—"and I conducted perhaps the grandest experiment of my storied career. Behold!" And we once again behold, because this well-trained Constance-wearing beast has descended the stairs, trailing a smear of slime on the velvet carpet. "Friends, I present... Re-Constance!"

"Shoulda called it 'Monstance'!" cackles the town's oh-so-pleased-with-herself librarian.

<<<*I am a Stardweller*>>>, gurgles the creature in pink. Bile and mouse intestines dribble from its mouth.

Professor Brightfever turns to his wife/creation. In my many encounters with the professor, both public and private, this is the only time he has revealed unease. "Your name is *Re-Constance,*" he gently reminds this thing that is perhaps not so well-trained after all. He returns attention to the crowd, his face again beaming. "She's a tad forgetful. A...side effect of the procedure."

"Me Annabeth once 'ad 'er a side effect," shouts a farmer, proudly thumbing the woman beside him. "It were in 'er bum!"

He laughs.

His Annabeth laughs.

The creature laughs. It then wraps two ghastly tendrils around the farmer's and Annabeth's necks. The tendrils slither tighter, tighter, until the farm couple's heads pop right off. The tendrils skewer the heads mid-air, thrust them back, and stuff them under that heavy, pink skirt. Savage munching echoes from within.

The couple's blood-spurting bodies collapse to the marbled floor.

Mrs. Tafferty screams. Shouts and whimpers surround us. Pandemonium abounds as men, women, and children flee from something that is neither man, woman, nor child.

"Please," Professor Brightfever cries, voice adrift in the din. "No need to panic. Mere side effects!"

More fleshy tendrils dart from the dress, eager for sustenance.

The librarian is suffocated.

Mrs. Tafferty's eyes are gouged out and the remaining tobacco sucked from her mouth.

A grinning Handsome Pete explodes in every possible way.

I feel a shove to my torso as the mayoress pushes herself away, away from the madness, away from this creature that wears Constance Brightfever's face and dress but is not, not, *not* Constance Brightfever.

You, too, Simon, are knocked aside. Cast aside. But, as always, my sturdy arms are here. You land gently within them. Our eyes lock. We share a look. *Our* look. Would that it could continue forever.

But, of course, it cannot.

Nearby, Professor Brightfever's formerly bellowing voice begs for help.

"Let go of me, Ned!" you cry, jamming an elbow into my tender chest, that chest you idly caressed days ago. Stunned physically (but perhaps not emotionally), I release you. You rush away, calling "Professor Brightfever!"

It is the last thing you say.

~~~

It is midnight. The calamity eventually ended, as all Professor Brightfever's calamities eventually end. I stand in the College cemetery, shovel in hand, Constance's re-deceased body at my feet in bloody pink frills.

Hers is one among myriad bodies. The librarian's. Handsome Pete's. Mrs. Tafferty's. Yours.

I warned you Professor Brightfever would break you, my love. Like you, I was once his "precious pupil." And like you, I again find myself doing his bidding. Digging graves for his latest mistake, as I have dug for so many of his past mistakes. Agnes. Greta. Allisandra. Constance. All those wives reduced to "side effects."

The stars shine on your body, my Simon, broken and cast aside.

I think about that beast from beyond. It called itself *a* Stardweller. Not *the* Stardweller.

You are slender of frame.

I am sturdy of arms.

The professor's laboratory is so very close.

Perhaps it is time to create our own side effects.

Where you find cogs and gears, you are also likely to find eldritch cults & tentacles. But why is that? The works of HP Lovecraft are technically out of era for steampunk & Victoriana. I invited horror writer and academic Mary SanGiovanni to enlighten us on the topic of

Lovecraft's Legacy of Cosmic Horror

a guest editorial by *Mary SanGiovanni*

Although I believe an argument can be made for certain fiction predating H.P. Lovecraft's to be considered proto-cosmic horror, the genesis of the subgenre clearly originated with Lovecraft himself. Despite what many writers and editors have acknowledged as possible flaws in the mechanics of his writing, and perhaps even more amazingly, despite his unacceptably racist views on populations outside of the white, Anglo-Saxon Protestant communities with which he was familiar, his work has not only persisted in the canon of horror literature to present day, but has seen recent resurgence and a growth in popularity. I believe there are a number of reasons for this, and that ultimately, those reasons speak to a vibrance and evolution of the horror genre as a whole which is inspiring and encouraging.

Few Lovecraftian experts will deny that H. P. Lovecraft was racist beyond being a product of his time. Although some evidence shows that toward the end of his life, as he travelled more extensively, corresponded more widely, and became aware of the earliest atrocities perpetrated by the Nazi party in Germany, his views softened considerably, it's clear that he thought the integration of diverse people into American society was a road to the dismantling of civilization. The question has often arisen whether these views were a result of true hatred for Jews, Asiatic peoples, and those of color, who served as a basis for some of his more loathsome "degraded" cultist characters. Some have argued that xenophobia —an actual fear of those not like him, which, throughout his life, reached near panic level—fueled his nightmare sense of the "Other" and his terror at the thought of exclusion and banishment from the safety, health, and security of the "civilized" world, a world he saw with dismay as changing too quickly for him.

Change—that, to me, is a key factor worth examining. When one looks at Lovecraft's upbringing and the series of sudden, tragic events that resulted in increasingly worse change in his life circumstances, it seems clear that any event which intruded on his sense of security and fomented change was something Lovecraft sought to avoid. I think fear of change ignited both sentiments in him—fear of unknown cultures encroaching on and ultimately replacing his own, and hatred of those who were, as he saw it, forcing that change upon the world. I don't think this in any way excuses his views or the awful things he said and wrote in correspondence to others as a result of those views. However, I do think that examining the true nature of his thought processes helps us understand the nature of his creations and the lasting impression those creations have had on the horror genre.

Lovecraft is famously quoted as saying, "The oldest and strongest emotion of mankind is fear, and the oldest and strongest kind of fear is fear of the unknown." *("Supernatural Horror in Literature," 1927).* I think he honestly believed this, deep in the core of his being. Change opens the door to the unknown, and while this is a primal fear, to one extent or another, in all of humanity, I think that for Lovecraft, this fear of change, this fear of the unknown that change would bring, was as much a terror in the microcosm of his personal existence as it was on the grander scheme of the universe. And in my opinion, the fear of change and the fear of the unknown (if not his reasons for that fear), are what have imbued his work with a universal appeal that has allowed the subgenre he created to evolve and flourish.

I think many people who are not particularly well-read in cosmic horror know it more for its perceived limitations than its actual limitless possibilities. Lovecraft stuck to a very specific set of criteria in his own work. Antiquated language, character stereotypes, cults, ancient tomes of forbidden magic, and other Lovecraftian tropes, at this point almost belie the subgenre's true horror, particularly in melodramatic adaptations which often fail to grasp fully its most prominent themes.

When cosmic horror is done well, it is a genre of *change*—of fluidity, of transformation, and of pervasive threat at such an alien and cosmic level that it inspires in humankind a sense of nihilistic despair. Our minds, our bodies, our very sense of time and space and reality as we know it are all subject to change, and are simply playthings for far greater powers. Even death is often not a reprieve for the indifference or outright malice that results from contact with these powers. Anything so far above and beyond human experience is often attributed to the realm of gods and goddesses, and it has always been humanity's nature to devote oneself slavishly to worshipping or preventing the influence of godlike entities, depending on whether we embrace the idea of change or not.

This leads to what I believe is an important element of the staying power that Lovecraft's work, and beyond that, cosmic horror in general, possesses. The evolution of science and technology, no matter how advanced, always seems to draw the minds and imaginations of people back to the spiritual, the supernatural. I think we, as a species, fear that someday science and technology will render the mysteries of the universe to cold facts, that things like the soul, the afterlife, why we love, why we find courage, *et cetera*—things which we hold up as ideals that transcend us—will be relegated to simple chemicals and processes. It would eliminate the magic and wonder many people need in their lives to find them worth living, to stave off the nihilism of a universe without them. This is why religion and spiritualism persist despite science. When we have surges of progress in science and technology, we immediately look for the questions and mysteries that arise from implementation of that progress. What will inter-planetary space travel mean for us? Who will we find out there? If we're not alone in the universe, how does that affect, enhance, or change religious stories of creation? When we see an evolution of medicine, we question future side effects. When new technolog-ical gadgets are developed, we look at the physical and especially psychological ramifications of social media and information ever ready at one's fingertips. When we progress as a society, we look to the supernatural in our speculative entertainment to reflect on some new mystery, some new question which we can strive to answer. I think we see a renewed appreciation of the speculative in general and of Lovecraft's type of fiction in particular whenever there is some conquer-ing of a universal mystery, something which for a time makes humanity just a little more superior and, perhaps, a little less in awe of the universe around us. However, that temporary superiority suggests, even for just a moment, that we might be alone, that all the magic of forces above and beyond us, looking out for us and guiding our fate, might not exist, and on some existential level, it's a lonely and terrifying thought. There is no solace, no security, no comfort to being alone in the universe. There is nowhere to look for answers, no one to pray to for help, should we need it. So we seek to rebalance that with entertainment that reminds us of all the magic as yet unexplained and mystery unanswered. Supernatural horror in general and cosmic horror specifically suits this need rather well. Lovecraft's work often is, at its core, stories about the possible repercussions of the pursuit of science and knowledge, and how the information discovered will change our whole perception of our universe and our place in it. One of the most horrific takeaways for some readers in Lovecraft's longer work, *At the Mountains of Madness,* is not the discovery of alien lifeforms of antiquated origin, but of the fact that their presence, and that of those who came before, suggests that humanity was nothing more than a failed experiment, a plaything that old, indifferent gods had grown tired of. If such a thing were true, then all we put our faith in (such as an all-seeing, all-loving God) would be a lie.

Another lasting element of Lovecraft's work is the suggestion of other planes of existence and even other universes. As string theory and experiments with CERN bring us closer to proving the existence of alternate dimensions, the fiction which reflects what may well be waiting on the other side is of particular appeal. Paradoxically, modern society is very much steeped in reality and very much removed from it; we want our horror to have a basis in logic and science, an attachment to the real world, however fantastical its other elements are. We watch reality shows, look for gritty realism in our fantasy, and want things to happen in real time, and yet so much of our "reality" is filtered through the skewed, distorted dream-lens of social media, internet search results, and online echo-chambers. In a sense, cosmic horror captures in fiction what we often see in our modern lives—a pursuit of truth which, once learned, we may wish we never knew, and a sense of reality which is not stable or consistent in our own lives, let alone across the span of humanity.

Another renewable appeal of Lovecraft's legacy is, I think, due to the modern entertainment environment. Books compete for the time and attention of the average consumer against television, movies, video games, and apps on the cell phone. So much visual media floods households with the tap of a button that many creators have had to rethink how they approach their craft. For writers, the competition to stay relevant has taken a two-pronged approach.

Firstly, writers have examined the subject matter of their horror. Classic monsters have always served as psychological symbols—of our fear of being different, of our fear of losing control of our bodies or minds, our fear of losing inhibition, of disease or disfigurement, of mindless consumerism, of insanity, of guilt, etc. The forms these symbols have taken in classic horror literature were often simple, effective representations of problems tackled by teens growing up, people afraid of war escalation and ultimate annihilation, scientists afraid of the retaliation of the flora and fauna of a planet we should have taken better care of, etc. However, as we evolve and mature, both individually and as a species, we recognize complexities in our persistent existence on the earth which require more fluid and perhaps, sometimes less tangible symbols. We process our fears and work out our solutions through monster stories, and as the world around us changes, so too do the problems we encounter and must solve. I think cosmic horror, the monsters of which have always been so much less predictable (and describable), frequently fit the bill as representations of the most difficult and least tangible experiences we seek to understand and process. They often represent change in a world which is rapidly changing exponentially all around us every day.

The second prong of the approach has been in seeing the evolution of the delivery methods of entertainment itself. I think writers have adapted not just their aethstetic in content but their range of content types to streaming services, digital formats, audio formats—in fact, adaptations in multiple formats, for every type of consumer. We are no longer just book writers, but potentially content source writers for television, movies, series, video games, comic books, graphic novels, merchandising, and more. And with the success of properties like the TV-adapted *Lovecraft Country* and the movie adaptation of Lovecraft's own *Colour Out of Space,* I think the producers of multimedia are seeing potential to bring a wider range of viewers content which is new and impressive and yet, at its substrate, psychologically familiar and meaningful. We are capable now of special effects which can finally do the monsters of cosmic horror real justice, and for many there is an appeal in that alone. Mostly, though, the genre lends itself to a flexibility of storytelling which many indie filmmakers, finding newfound freedom to create with the most sophisticated tools of the trade finally available to them, are looking to explore in ways that, in the past, simply weren't possible.

The inclusion of Lovecraftian elements, particularly its mythology and monsters, in pop culture through toys, rock music, video games, movies, and television shows (*South Park*'s two-part Cthulhu episodes, for example) has introduced Lovecraft's work to new generations of fans outside of its traditional cult readership. Millenials, who have displayed a love for all things retro, from records to 1980s fashion to 8-bit video games, have access to the source materials for many of the obscure Lovecraftian references that appeal in their entertainment, and as generations will do, they have sought ways to repurpose and integrate the retro horror of Lovecraft into the tapestry of their pop culture. This is a testament to the transcendent appeal of cosmic horror, and with the current and upcoming generations of creators, I believe that appeal has been justified, in spite of or maybe because of Lovecraft's abhorrent views, through reclamation, often by the very groups of people Lovecraft would have held in contempt.

I believe the most prominent reason for the persistence of Lovecraft's legacy, not just in modern horror but in pop culture in general, is its potential for evolution. I have always believed that speculative fiction genres were the perfect vehicles for exploring the more human experiences. To accommodate the full essence of these experiences, you need genres which are flexible enough to experiment and to reach for places that fiction in the past had yet to go. I feel that horror, especially—a genre which is, itself, born of emotion—is the perfect way to examine such a wide range of experiences, and that cosmic horror can manage the psychological, the emotional, the visceral, the esoteric, and the spiritual all in one story, if need be. I think a lot of modern writers, particularly in an era that is recognizing the importance of diversity and inclusion, are, in an almost ironic twist, finding that Lovecraft's framework is allowing them to customize horror fiction to accommodate their world views and personal or cultural experiences through cosmic horror's unique lenses and filters. Elements like the "Other" are being redefined and repurposed to fit a wider range of relatable fear experiences, while still holding true to the aspects which define cosmic horror as a subgenre. Tropes are being subverted. The very nature of cosmic horror is evolving and growing, shaping and reshaping without losing the substance which defines it. In essence, new writers with new perspectives and experiences are expanding it in multiple directions, telling varied and exciting stories through ancient eyes. I mentioned before that of all the elements that define cosmic horror, to me, the most persistent are the sense of cosmic grandness in terms of the antagonistic force, the idea of transformation, and the flexibility and fluidity of the true nature of the universe. The very structure of the genre encompasses those same things in its composition.

The lasting legacy of Lovecraft's work is most evident in this current resurgence in popularity of cosmic horror which has been, at length, discussed. As both a practitioner and fan, I believe this bodes well for horror fiction in general; we see readers coming to recognize the identifiable and relatable cosmic horror elements which fuel popular forms of entertainment. There is a distinctly legitimizing literary association with Lovecraft's work, and by that, I mean that Lovecraft's work is (or is finally being) recognized as classic literature, not simply a stream of the weird relegated to pulp magazines of a bygone era. There is a recognized legitimacy of the artistry in cosmic horror which gives credibility to horror as a whole. The flexibility of the subgenre, as well as its often cerebral themes and literary delivery, elevate the notion of horror fiction in general as artistic work capable of being profound, reflective, intellectual, emotionally moving, and accessible to an audience who might shy away from the horror label because of misguided genre perceptions of excessive violence and gore without substance. The evolution of the genre has caused a resulting evolution of the perception of the genre, which has led to an increase in readership. The vibrance of horror fiction relies on the innovation of creators, of course, but also the influx of new readers over time. Any subgenre which does both, as cosmic horror has done, is a boon to the horror genre as a whole.

Ultimately, cosmic horror's continued popularity is due to the fact that Lovecraft, despite his flaws, was able to develop a means of exploring universal fears of the "Other" and the "outside" that lends itself to the very nature of change while examining the horror behind it. He was able to ask the cosmic questions which trouble the soul, to raise doubts about our origins, our existence, and perhaps most importantly, our place in the universe. These fears may change shape, may wear new faces, but they have persisted since the beginning of humanity, and so continue to be a fertile source of inspiration for modern writers of cosmic horror. Lovecraft's legacy is, perhaps ironically, in creating a subgenre of supernatural horror fiction, the fantastic and weird, which can develop to include diverse viewpoints and multiple stories. Like the entities of his mythos, cosmic horror is a vast conglomeration of experiences, a multitude of eyes perceiving the world, of mouths telling stories, and of the dark, tentacled appendages of ideas beyond the ability of simple human understanding. It is a genre which will continue to grow, evolve, assimilate, incorporate, and for those of us who are fans, to continue to terrify for aeons to come.

Lena Ng

The Monstrous Metronome

HE WORDS strangled my heart. I was sick—sick at the unbridled venom released upon me as I read the crawling black-and-white slander in typeset, disparaging my work. I, Leon Klein, concert pianist extraordinaire, who has dedicated my life to practice, practice, and more practice, who has devoted my whole being, my whole soul, to the craft of music, read the critiques of last night's concert. *Tepid. Conservative. Clearly past the prime of his career.*

The most bilious of the critiques harkened from the odious Helmut Archfecken from *The Herald's Tribune.* This critic did not write, but spilled acid from his pen. He had never cared for my work; he was a beady-eyed, weasel-mouthed man who could never build, only destroy. Despite the intellectual nature of his work, he had the physique of a butcher. He dealt in hyperbole, in cruelty, was paid by each acerbic word to dismantle a lifetime's work.

A small, sickening excerpt:

Leon Klein, whom I will admit had shown flashes of genius in his youth, with last night's performance, instead of aging like fine wine, has turned into vinegar. His playing has descended into an insufferable air of complacency, self-satisfaction, and obvious choices, without the whimsy of attack in the high range and little energy in the low…

A short piece, but stinging, as though he would not waste words denouncing the performance. I would not have these words be my legacy. In the twilight of my years, I will have vindication. I will perform what no musician has been able to perform: I will play in concert, in one sitting, the piece that no other pianist, living or dead, has been able to play live in front of an audience. Raspuninsky's *Magnum clavicembalisticum* which requires over three hours of virtuoso playing, spread over eight, focused, gruelling movements. It is said that in the final movement, the last two pages are so technically demanding, so technically terrifying, the joints of the hand grind down in its practice—the counterpoint wears down the bones like pumice on clay. One segment, known as 'The Devil's Minefield,' includes blind leaps of the left hand played at an insane staccato speed. It was said the composer had made a Faustian bargain in order to spawn this opus, his only work to remain strangely unscathed after his house had burned to the ground. His body was never recovered. It was rumoured the devil came in person to collect him.

The *Magnum*, also known as the 'Yellow Song' at the fear it strikes, was a concerto many musicians have decided never to attempt, not even to gaze over the printed music. For some, the lingering horror of its effect on the prodigy Josef von Gieseking prevented them from endeavouring to play the piece. I had heard snippets of the song, from failed efforts from multitudes of up-and-comers who thought this could be a way to make a name for themselves. No recording existed of the finale—an infernal *presto con fuoco,* the fastest speed one could play, which needed both a limber fluidity and precision despite a breakneck speed.

I have been challenged by pieces before, stretched to the limits of perfection and obsession. If the song would drive me mad, no matter. After the last review, I would never draw the acclaim I had in my youth. The *Magnum* would be my swan song. I would perform it or die.

I could hear the blood drain from my agent's face when I telephoned him with my plans.

It was several moments before he spoke, and when he did, he could not hide his trepidation in his voice.

"I applaud your ambition," he said. "Your risk-taking, your determination, especially at your age and this late stage of your career." A heavy pause, dubious. "But you know, no musician has ever completed the piece. The most we have is composites. Snatches of bars, of motifs. Only the composer was able to finish the song in its entirety. And the rumour, ridiculous as they may be, was that he…he…"

"Sold his soul to the devil," I finished. "Preposterous. Ludicrous. As though man has a soul to sell."

"Yes, I'm well aware of your views of humanity, your nihilism. Whatever the stories may be, no one has ever performed the song in concert; to have you try it is folly. Utter hubris."

"I'm sure this is the same advice given to Sir Edmund Hillary. Without risk, he would have no reputation. I will play it because it is there." I hung up the phone.

♪♪♪

The Royal Conservatory of Music's researcher, a milquetoast man, gave me a long, squinting look when I requested the piece. He made a phone call and directed me to the fifth floor of the archives, filled with the musty scent of arcane knowledge, with music dating back to the origin of the form. The librarian gave a smirky little half-smile with an arched brow as I collected the music. No doubt she had heard of the multitude of failed attempts by overly ambitious students who sought to make a name for themselves. She disappeared into the stacks and after some agonizing minutes, returned with the treasure. I clutched the pages to my chest as I returned home.

♪♪♪

The beginning phrases were deceptively simple, exquisitely elegant. I could feel a slow electric current travelling up the planes of my hands, down my arms, infusing over my spine. An elongated largo, approximately sixty beats a minute, the pace of a heart at rest. As I played, a languid trance seemed to come over me, as though the music was transporting me to another dimension of existence. My hands seemed to take over and my mind was free to wander. I saw the drifting hills of Arenda's Pass and heard the calls to prayer from the spiraled, looming temples. The percussive waves would build and fall, white froth lingering on the abandoned shores.

I wept as the dream broke when my fingers could not follow the music's path. Each day, I would begin again, slower, then faster, then a missed note, a misplayed phrase, and the structure would tumble. I gnashed my teeth at each abrupt wrench from the musical dream. My hands clenched into fists as I would crash them into the keys with frustration.

Weeks went by, then months and I was no nearer to the song's completion. I dreamed of the *Magnum* in my sleep, pounding the piano's ivory keys as the flames leapt and danced while my house burned down around me.

My agent came around with more talk to dissuade me. He saw the look in my eye and sat on the corner of the couch. I played what I could and the notes became a discordant mess. My agent sat frozen with a dazed look in his eyes. For a long time, he remained silent, gnawing his thumbnail with worry heavy upon his face. When he seemed to see me, he discussed in length—haltering at first, then more impassioned —the song's dangerous appeal. The sin of such music, music which could arrest your soul and hypnotize you into doing its bidding; music which could pull the emotion from the most hardened of hearts and release it into the sky. He left before the sun rose.

One night, dark outside for many hours, with eyes red from exhaustion, beard grey and tangled and body sprawled over the keyboard, I cried out, "Oh God, help me. Let me conquer this piece. My labour, my effort, my deepest pride and humility, I offer to you. If I have a soul, I offer it to you." I collapsed, sheets of music drifting from the stand to the floor.

The next morning, I made a strong pot of coffee. Instead of gulping it down, I slowly sipped it, with deep breathing and repeating a silent mantra to strengthen my resolve. I sat again at the piano. With slow, meticulous repetition, the middle section took audible form. The arching phrases, the ingenious, soaring motifs that hid in the black-barred clefs before revealing themselves in a process of wondrous unveiling. Although the notes seemed to be a tangle of cacophony, in a swarm of black dots organized by horizontal lines on the page, I began to understand, to hear the composer's dark, pleading vision. It was a musical prayer of sorts. A begging prayer, a desperate prayer, a musical shield to ward off all the things that lay beyond. As though the composer thought to stave off decay with a melodious path through the confusion of life. My head swam with elusive harmonies and my hands ached from longing.

Finally, after hundreds of hours of practicing, I felt ready to start the eighth and final movement: The Devil's Minefield. I decided to approach the piece through the Madowski method—the practice of taking each bar slowly, engraining each note into muscle memory until perfection was achieved before attacking the next. After ten weeks, I progressed through the first ten bars. My hands ached, which affected the parts of the music I had thought I had mastered, and my face grew pallid from lack of sunlight.

After a particularly gruelling session, my eyes raw and knuckles throbbing, I looked to the darkness of the sky. "I called to you, O Lord, and you refused to answer. In my hour of need, you have abandoned me. From now on, I will turn my face away from you. Instead of looking above, I will look below. If you can not help me, I'll now look to your enemy for aid. As you have spurned me, I will spurn you.

"Lord of Darkness, Lucifer, Satan, Beelzebub, the horrors of the underworld, I now beseech you. What I have offered to Him, I now offer to you. My soul is yours if I can play this piece!"

Outside, the rain beat upon my windows. An answering flash of light and crack of thunder. I heard the deep, mocking laugh of a thousand demons. *What have I done?* I shrank away from the piano, went to my bedroom, and sank into the corner of my bed.

A flood of sunlight filled my room. I awoke amidst a tangle of sheets. I touched my haggard face, my sunken chest, the length of my spindly legs. The day was the same as any other. I had woken whole, not struck down by last night's utterance of blasphemy. Could it have been a dream, the condemnation of God and my offer to serve the devil?

I dragged myself to my ivoried captor. The piano keys seemed hateful to me now. Before I could approach the instrument in the spirit of music's construction. Now I saw it as the future of my destruction. The pages of the eighth movement stared at me, conquered me. I attacked and retreated, made slight progress before being beaten back, massaged my temples and rubbed my enfeebled, obstinate hands until the sun's cooling rays began to drift into the horizon. I thrust myself away from the keyboard. The pent-up frustration led to pacing, and in a creative impotent rage, I made my way from the house and skulked into the soot-covered cobbled streets of the city.

It was his weird eye that caught me. Though it was through glass, his goatish eye stopped me in my tracks. The window display showed such eccentric goods of gears and brass. Machines which could create an electric current with the turning of a wheel. Tin toys with faded paint on their harlequin costumes. Droopy-headed marionettes which hung limply from their restraints.

So many peculiar things, sinister things, it could

have been the devil's own odds-and-ends shop, with items befitting his fireplace mantel. In the corner of the display, a carved wooden contraption, triangular in shape, held my attention. A metronome, in gleaming teak, with strange engravings like evil omens over the entirety of its surface.

The shop's door creaked as I entered the darkened emporium. The air smelled of age and oppression. The curiosities were crammed everywhere—on shelves to the ceiling, behind the counter, even haphazardly on the floor. I could have examined more closely the murky jars and encased porcelains but instead I pointed to the window display.

The weird-eyed proprietor, who had the squat physique of a goblin with a heavy jaw to match, gave me a leering smile like he held a perverse secret. He picked up the metronome and gave it to me for inspection. The wood of the device felt warm, almost alive, with its dormant heart inside. He pointed out a marking—did I not recognize the Crimson Sign?

He tapped the tangled marking. "Why do you want it?"

"For the *Magnum clavicembalisticum*."

He cackled as he declared I was mad.

I could have placed my hands around his neck and strangled him right there. Instead, I wound my trembling fingers into a knot and asked him why he would say this.

"I know of the scandals that composition had created, the denouncements by the ruling class, the condemnations by the clergy. The disappearance of its composer, the handwritten parchment pages unscathed despite being surrounded by ash. The gibbering insanity of Josef von Gieseking. And other stories you may not have heard of, stories suppressed by the clandestine societies of occultant religions. I trade in mystical artifacts with these cults, hear murmurs of their secrets. The strange case of Uwe Wagner. I understand he had fallen, but why was he there? What happened to Klaus Hoffman's hands? To Günter Richter's eyes?"

I held tight around the metronome. His warnings were no use to me. They only strengthened my resolve.

He gave me a look that recognized obsession. "It calls to you." He lowered his voice. "This metronome is the catalyst. It is the key to dimensions of which you have never dreamed. Its past is shrouded in mystery. Who had carved its profane runes? Who had marked it with the Crimson Sign? Was its timber hewn from the Wood of the Suicides? It has burned through generations of the infamous, musically genius Griminachis. Madness runs through that family, the presence of the metronome dismissed as a strange coincidence. It is also said that with the metronome's hypnotic beat, instead of time being your master, with this device, you will master time."

We haggled over the price and of course I paid dearly.

At home, I placed the metronome on the piano, removed the cover, and wound the device with the accompanying silver key. I ran the tips of my fingers over the strange carvings which resembled a Rorschach drawing—disembodied eyes, a coil of boneless limbs, wisps of tangled hair. I set the speed to allegro, a decent speed but not nearly as fast as the piece was written to be played.

Instead of concentrating on the music, I listened to the metronome's beat. It had a hypnotic rhythm, and in a trance, my hands were flying over the keyboard, dancing over the minefield, leaping over the flames. The notes pounded in my head, taking me on a journey. I flew over the soaring cliffs of Viskyai, where hoards of winged creatures nested. I dove into the underwater Caves of Nystothmolan, where the volcanic eruptions sent currents through the waters.

Lost in the flow of the music, of its own volition, the metronome seemed to speed up. My hands played faster, faster, not my own hands any more, but the tool of some dark god. In time with the beat, my heart thumped in my chest and the sweat trickled down my red face to drip from my jaw. My hands leapt from one end of the keyboard to the other. With other concertos, my one hand would know where to go while I could keep an eye on the other. With this piece, however, my eyes would flicker between both hands as they bounded over the keys. Fluttering arpeggios, not in tandem, but in maddening counterpoint. Abrupt key changes, abrupt time changes, odd numbers juxtaposed against even. Syncopated rhythms, atonal motifs which didn't reveal their meaning until the final thunderous passage, the hammer of the metronome driving me onwards.

I would fall asleep in my bed, but awoke with my hands over the keys, the music, the metronome's drum invading my dreams. I knew that sound well. It was the pulsing of the metronome, the counting down of life's seconds, the beating of my old man's heart.

Now as I played, a feeling unfamiliar swelled in my chest and moved into my throat. It tasted of triumph.

My agent dropped by unannounced. There must have been a wildness to my face since he couldn't help but shrink back. "Have you been eating? Sleeping?" he asked, instead of asking how I was.

"Listen," I said, "for you are about to witness history." I sat him on the duchess chair so I could watch his astonishment. He furrowed his brow as I released the metronome's tang. With its beat guiding the way, from my hands flowed music and opened the windows into the uncanny. We began a journey over skyways and seas. I felt the singe of the stars, the foam and flash of oceans trembling.

But something was wrong and I felt my hands tiring. I gnashed my teeth. I felt the condescending gaze of my agent upon me, his heavy silence as he sat bolted upon the chair.

Just as I was about to start the Devil's Minefield…

"Stop!" said my agent, shooting up from the chair. "Don't you see that horrible thing glaring?"

The music was broken, and an uncontrollable

sensation of hatred seized me. All my work, all my art, all my concentration poorly heeded. A vortex of emotions exploded from within. I hated this man more than I have ever hated anyone. I sprang up from the bench. His eyes bulged as he felt my strong pianist's hands around his neck. I squeezed until I heard something break. My clenched hands relaxed and I spent the rest of the evening digging a grave.

I felt no remorse, and later, slept like the dead.

♪♪♪

The night of the concert was upon me. An unusual set-up—within the piano bench, noise muffled to be heard only by my ears, the metronome, muted, ticked away. The concert hall was full; I spotted the odious critic, Helmut Archfecken, seated in the left wing. Despite the tuxedo, he still resembled a butcher. His face looked both bloated and smug, like he ate too much cream. I wanted to wipe the gloat from his face.

I walked to the centre of the stage, my polished shoes gleaming under the lights, and took a deep bow. I pushed back the tails of my tuxedo as I sat on the velveteen bench. Within the bench, I hear the soft ticking, like the sound of a wristwatch. I paused for only a moment and then I began.

The beginning lulled the audience with its largo melody and elongated phrases. The metronome's pace quickened as I moved through the middle movements, rivulets of sweat dripping from my reddened face to my collar. The melodic phrases brought me to the days of the continental shift, the movement of the land as it shuddered over the planet. It led me to the deepest part of the ocean where the sightless sea creatures gibbered and glowed.

The tick of the metronome and suddenly I was distracted. From the corner of my eye, I glimpsed —*Lord, forgive me!*—the maggot-white face of my agent. He grinned at me with a lipless sneer. The audience, I realized with a start, was that of the damned. There, in the corner, sat Josef von Gieseking. His mouth opened and out emerged a swollen coffin worm which squirmed against his mottled lips. There, in the third row, sat Klaus Hoffman, splaying the mutilation of his hands. In an aisle seat sat Günter Richter who watched my performance with segmented eyes.

Helmut Archfecken stretched the black wings which had punctured through the back of his tight-fitting tuxedo.

Finally, the end was nigh. The eighth movement was fast approaching, the dreaded Devil's Minefield. Both hands attacked the keys, leaping, soaring, hands inhumanly wild. The metronome's ticking, the ticking, the infernal ticking! Speeding up, faster than *presto con fuoco,* faster than fury, driving the swiftness of my heart. Whipping me like the backs of galloping horses. Like the red shoes of the doomed ballerina who was sentenced to death by dance, despite the exhaustion and fear, I was glued to the piano keys, fingers hurtling over white keys and black.

A crushing weight bloomed in my chest. Shallow, laboured breaths. A strange, acrid smell of brimstone. Sweat turned into blood, seeped from my pores. A frightening lightning of pain struck through my jaw, along my left arm, radiating from the ribs to my back. The metronome's pounding, relentless beat drove me onward. I could no more leave the keys to clutch at my chest in agony than a man release an electrified wire.

Tongues of fire danced around the stage, screamed its heated language. The theatre was burning around me. The shrieks as the audience joined in. The smell of roasting flesh polluted the air. The perfume of suffering! The passion! The horror! This was no longer a concert, but a grotesque scene from the blood-soaked Grand Guignol.

I played louder to drown out the screaming. With each leap of my hands during the Devil's Minefield, with a heart-stabbing twang, the piano strings started snapping. Slicing sounds thrummed through the air. Stabbing pain where the piano wires hooked into my hands, my shoulders, punctured through my polished shoes until I resembled a musician turned marionette.

What happened to my eyes?

Blinded by blood, I heard infernal laughing as the song's prayer was answered. Now he was here to collect. I felt his presence shambling up the steps to the stage. Now he stood at the top of the stairs. I heard his squelching glide across the platform. Nearer and nearer, he came. Now he was at the end of the piano. I smelled the breath of decay. I felt a bloated palm brush my skin, the branding of the Sign into my neck.

I don't know how much time has passed. Centuries perhaps? The blink of an eye? Hellfire burns in the fireplace. On its mantel, I am the central display. I hear the clicking turn of a metal key. Fresh pain as the pull of piano wire strings cause my hands to start moving.

For his amusement, the Devil's Minefield, his favourite part, I will play for eternity.

Kaffeeklatsch

with **Lena Ng** *and* *Andrew McCurdy*

Andrew: Lena, to begin, thank you for taking part in the Curiosities Kaffeeklatsch, the section in each edition where we chat with one of our authors.

Lena: Thank you very much, Andrew. I am so pleased and flattered to be selected for this chat.

Andrew: I loved the narration for "The Monstrous Metronome". Despite the mania and questionable deals, there was something relatable in the protagonist's insecurities. How did you come up with the idea behind the story?

Lena: I've always thought it was interesting that there

is a disconnect between reading music reviews and listening to the music itself. No matter how well the music is described, you can't get a sense of what it actually sounds like until you hear it. I was inspired to write a story that would leave the reader curious enough to want to seek out the music and listen to it, although it doesn't exist outside the page.

Other than that, the story is a confluence of influences and I hope readers will have fun spotting them.

For theme: the movies *Black Swan* and *The Wrestler* —following one's obsessions over a cliff.

For the piano piece: *The King in Yellow* with reference to a creative work which drives the performer insane.

Deal with the Devil trope—usually the protagonist can get out of the contract through a literal interpretation of the wording so I went for a 'Be careful what you wish for' ending.

Lovecraft: strange geography and history before the dawn of man

Thomas Ligotti: marionettes and automatons

Edgar Allan Poe: first-person, 'you may think I'm mad' flawed protagonist

When writing about the music, I could be as descriptive as I liked since I was inventing a piece. It was very freeing.

Andrew: I'll admit, I was caught up in the mania of the music, I wanted to hear the *Yellow Song* as I was reading, at times I imagined I could. Your descriptions of the musical elements rang true. Do you have a background in music and did you have to do much research in writing this?

Lena: Growing up, I studied classical piano for ten years through the Royal Conservatory of Music and was just terrible at it. I didn't appreciate classical music at the time (though now I enjoy it) and had no passion for it. My late father loved classical music and my mother believed in never quitting something started so I continued with these lessons despite my lack of talent.

When I practiced, I always thought my metronome was cursed. Why was it speeding up? Why was it slowing down? Why couldn't I play in time or fast enough? It had to be the metronome's fault, of course. All that is left of those lessons is the vocabulary, I'm afraid, since my hands have atrophied into mittens. To get a sense of how music is described, I read a few music reviews and jumped in.

Andrew: A little tangential, do you listen to music when you write, or do you find it distracting?

Lena: I have some fear of the blank page so I find music helps me to relax enough to get into the flow. Once I'm in the depths of writing, however, I completely tune out the music.

Andrew: In preparation for this chat, I reread "The Finishing School", your story that appeared in the previous edition of *Curiosities*. I've read it a few times now, and still, it has a sense of the unexpected about it. The oft repeated warning at the school: *Don't let the cat out!* makes me laugh, especially after we've met the cat. The story was included in our *Uncategorized Collections* issue. Since we copped out, how would you describe, and categorize that story?

Lena: I was going for weird and surreal. I was reading Robert Aickman's *Cold Hand in Mine* and found it horribly creepy with much going on beyond the page. So I tried to write a story using a similar technique—letting the reader attempt to deduce what was happening instead of being blatant about it. I was trying to write a weird satire on the socialization of girls into womanhood which came out more funny than creepy. I would still like to attempt a creepy version of this theme someday. Tone sometimes gets away from me—it's easier for me to write comedy than horror. If I find it funny, I'm pretty sure the reader will find it funny. I'm never really sure, however, if something is scary—since I already know what is about to happen, I'm not afraid or in suspense so I can't rely on my gut to tell me if I'm getting the desired effect. So I lean on technique and hope for the best.

Andrew: I enjoyed the comedic and the weird elements in both stories. What are your thoughts on the relationship between horror and comedy?

Lena: I think comedy can be a defensive mechanism against some of the absurdities of life. If you don't laugh, you'll cry, right? It can pull us out of helplessness and unfreeze us into taking action.

Andrew: Tell me about some of your other writing.

Lena: I have stories seeded all over the place in all kinds of genres. I'm hoping to gain readers one story at a time. Many of my stories are available to read online in *Zooscape* (animal stories), *Hybrid Fiction* (horror-comedy) or in free PDF magazines such as *Polar Borealis* (Canadian content), *Sage Cigarettes,* and *The Quiet Reader.* I've self-published an ebook short story collection called *Under an Autumn Moon.* I've also written a novel, a Gothic romance, that I've been submitting for publication.

Andrew: What appeals to you most about writing, and what impression would you like people to get from your work?

Lena: I like the challenge of creating something purely from imagination. To create emotion out of black-and-white words on a page. There seems to be something mystical and magical about how writing can affect the reader. I want readers to be entertained and to feel something at the same time—to laugh, or be puzzled, or creeped out, or in suspense. I want the story to linger after the last sentence is read. I want the story to stick to the mind, just like good food can stick to the ribs.

Andrew: I'm nodding in agreement, reading absolutely affects the reader; it may be fictional, but it's also a communication of ideas and emotion from one person to another. How do you think writing affects the writer?

Lena: Writing exposes the vast internal world of the writer, clarifies the thought processes, organizes and pinpoints the nebulous emotional moments and opinions of that particular time and place. It unearths the hidden.

Andrew: What are some of the challenges to marketing your work?

Lena: Marketing? What's that? I'm a digital hermit so I'm asocial. But I do belong to a bunch of writers groups and spread the word through email lists. A list of my publications can be found on Goodreads and on Amazon. I write in different genres so I would think marketing me as a specific type of writer would be difficult. A reader who likes my horror stories might feel disappointed with reading my children's stories or romances. Or, more optimistically, delighted.

Andrew: Is there a specific genre that you like to read, or authors that inspire you?

Lena: Right now, I like reading weird stories. The

weirder, the better. I love so many authors that we could be here forever. Angela Carter, for her rich, evocative prose. Kafka for his matter-of-fact surrealism. Brian Evenson for his unexplained story concepts. Leonora Carrington for humour mixed in with the strange. The heart-felt metaphors of Oliver Sacks and the lyrical sentences of Patrik Svensson. I'm self-taught as a writer, and these authors are a few of my teachers.

Andrew: Thanks again for joining me for the Kaffeeklatsch, I look forward to reading more of your stories. Cheers, Lena, the last word is yours.

Lena: I love your publication and hope more of my stories will grace its pages. I feel like it was such a fluke getting my two stories in. Lightning has already struck twice so what are my chances in the future? I hope I can write more stories that will catch at your imagination.

Deborah L. Davitt

To Our Own Ghosts

ICHAEL WENTWORTH could hear voices coming from the nursery. His wife Emily's, raised in agitation. The baby's, rising in a low wail.

And…something else. Lower. Colder. Crueler.

Tea-cup still in hand, he made his way upstairs. He didn't tap on the door. While the wall-papered room should have been warmed by the steam radiator creaking gently against the wall, cold air blasted past him through the door as he opened it.

Over his wife's shoulder, bared to nurse their son, he spotted a shadowy female figure standing near the window, wearing an old black gown that had seen better days. A widow's veil, the likes of which he hadn't seen since he was a boy, drifted over her features, concealing every detail. His heart hammered at the intrusion…but part of him had expected this.

They'd been warned, hadn't they, when they'd bought this house.

"You don't scare me." Emily raised her chin, her short-bobbed curls barely touching her shoulders as she did.

Michael watched as the figure lifted its veil. Tilted its face into the dim light of the electric bulbs burning near Emily's chair, revealing a desiccated visage and empty eye-sockets filled with blood that leaked down her cheeks like tears.

In Emily's arms, their son wailed again, waving his tiny fists.

"You think I haven't seen worse?" Emily demanded. "I nursed my family through the influenza outbreak in 1918. I watched my brothers and sisters turn blue and die. I helped in the casualty wards, listening to men gasp for air after their lungs had been ravaged by mustard gas. You can't hurt me. Go *away.*"

The ghost raised a finger, pointing menacingly at Emily and the child. *You neglect your son,* it hissed.

The cold whisper crawled up Michael's spine. Slid along the walls. Tapped at the frosted window. "Emily," he said mildly. "Why don't you give me Thomas? You have a meeting tonight, don't you?"

Emily looked away from the ghost, her expression surprised as she registered his presence for the first time. "Michael! Darling!" She pulled her dress up a little self-consciously as she stood, her back to the looming apparition. Michael kept an eye on the specter warily. Just in case its clawed hands reached out for her. "You don't mind my going out?" A hint of uncertainty in her voice as her eyes edged to the side. As if the ghost's words had shaken her, despite her bravado.

"Certainly not. Thomas and I can have a jolly gent's night together." He took the infant in his free arm, nestling the small head against his shoulder. "Besides, I happen to agree with you on the whole question of suffrage, and you need a break from Thomas now and again." He pressed a kiss to her forehead. "Go do some good."

A hiss from the spirit made Emily's face twitch. "Is it *there?*" she whispered. "Is it real, or am I imagining—"

"Oh, I see it. We *were* warned when we moved in. Run along. I'll have a chat with our uninvited guest. See if I can work things out, eh?"

Emily laughed, the low, ringing sound he loved so much. "And if you can manage that, more people should retain you for your services as a barrister."

"They should," he agreed equitably, taking her seat in the chair, regarding the spirit.

As the door closed behind Emily, the spirit hissed again and raised its claws, trying to reach for the infant on his shoulder. "Stop that," Michael informed the ghost tiredly. "I spent four years in the trenches of the Western Front. I saw my closest friends die, choking on their own blood. You don't scare me any more than you frightened Emily."

The spirit twitched back, clearly befuddled. *You neglect your child—*

Michael glanced sidelong at the infant now firmly dozing on his shoulder, and took a sip of his tea. "No. Just because we're raising him differently than you raised yours, and just because Emily isn't a martyr to his upbringing, doesn't make us neglectful. Try again."

Trespassers! This is my house! Mine!

"No," Michael replied stolidly, reaching up to adjust the shade on the electric lamp, "we purchased this house. Our names are on the deed. That makes *you* a trespasser—or at the least, a tenant who's damned well in arrears in terms of rent. Pay up or there's a bottle of holy water downstairs. Beside the rat poison and the fire extinguisher, I believe." He believed in being prepared. So did Emily.

The ghost recoiled, starting to weep. *I lost them. I lost all of them, because of my own inattention—you're making a terrible mistake—*

Michael sighed. "I understand. You feel that you have unfinished business. But this isn't your place anymore. It's not your time. We've got electricity now, and plenty of our own evils to deal with. Why don't you move on?"

You'll regret this, she whispered. *There's worse than me—*

Michael exhaled, remembering the hundreds of

spirits climbing out of the trenches, clambering through the barbed wire hell of no man's land to take the hands of equally-ghostly enemies before vanishing before his eyes. Those nights in Belgium lurked behind his eyelids every night. Along with all the faces of those he'd lost. He didn't doubt that Emily saw similar things before sleep, herself. "I don't doubt that," he replied, his throat tightening. "But they're at least *our* ghosts to deal with. Leave us to it."

The ghost retreated, for the moment. Michael didn't doubt for an instant that she'd be back to pester some other lodger. Or even little Thomas, once the baby grew older. "The trick is," he counseled his son softly, "learning to live with all your own ghosts. Owning your guilt for still numbering among the living."

The baby hiccupped, and Michael kissed his son's soft forehead. "It's all right. You'll learn, yourself. In time. Though I hope you won't need to."

Marisca Pichette

The Revellers

N THE GLOAMING of the year, when trees' bark shrinks and holds fast to the mighty trunk; when the life-filled woods are stripped of those merry, clamorous sounds which bespeak a nature of anything but gloom; when all the shade-giving leaves are robbed from the canopy and replaced instead with an ever-present atmosphere of shade-ridden air, oppressive and dank; when nature's flesh becomes bone, and New England sheds her bitter skin—just in this darkest, dreariest time—I am accustomed to make a journey to visit my uncle. He lives not far from my house, in the nestled hills to the north, where the lonesome winter is always close, and

need but extend a finger to claim the region in ice and snow, no matter the season.

It was at the advent of such a visit, when November was fast waning, and the light had gradually withdrawn from the chilling sky, that glacial clouds moved in, washing the grey land in a different, negative light. This sable glow suffused my home, creeping on mummer's feet to inhabit every inch, like a bad-tempered, immovable squatter with intentions to stay for an indefinite period. I have heard tell from many acquaintances of how the perishing season hangs low upon their mood, pressing heavily on their muscles and denying the mind of pleasurable thoughts—but I confess it had never seen fit to harass me in such a manner. In fact, it was a time of the year I looked to with patient nostalgia, delighting in the long hours of darkness, the better to focus my thoughts on intellectual matters, with little to distract me—save the occasional squawk of a migrating goose, or the crow's coarse cough.

Alas, no more! Now I await that portion of the year with intense, unmanageable *dread*. With terror do I behold the first leaf to quiver and fall, or watch the days grow steadily shorter and the warm light fade utterly away, leaving me in blackness. Sable, ebony and obsidian! These are the colours of that season of death, of demise. Oh, to have winter! The fantastic ice and snow, so white, so bright to my eyes! The cold that keeps me locked away those nights, and the sun that wakes me! Ah, for winter to come swiftly, and not to let this long age of falling, of rot and detritus persist. For it is the winding down of the clock, the stripping of the carcass that works such ruin on my fevered mind. I cannot—I will not—endure it again.

Even now, I feel that horror stealing upon me by inescapable degrees, even as the leaves stay fast on the branches, and the sun still beats on my shoulders. It is all in my mind—it must be!—for to admit it as real —oh, wicked horror! My uncle—oh!

As I put my pen to this page, I tremble to imagine the consequences my words may bring. Will they expose the truth for falsehood? Make the falsehood true? My thoughts are at odds with reality, my fancies governing my will. It cannot be true what I saw near a decade ago; and, in faith, I know my uncle to be alive, as I have sometimes received a letter from him—but not since that most disturbing happenstance have I ventured to his house. For I cannot—I will not—go back.

It was a day to champion night, wrapped in all the splendour of darkness and cold, but for the accident that it came when one could see and move about in its hefty berth. The condemned leaves scuttled across the ground, cackling and hissing as they went like so many awful hags. I took the road to my uncle's house with a calm and meditative air, on foot—though truly, the way was rather long for that, but I enjoyed the journey—and the sepulchral atmosphere did not agitate me then. As I said before, I was that wretch who did not fear the dark; rather, I relished in it, and saw nothing in the leaves' dreadful susurrus to upset my good humour.

Woe to he who ignores the signs, even as they parade across his path! That night in day's semblance… no sane man would have chosen it, as I did, for sauntering. In the long years since that day, I have never seen one like it, never one so absolute in midnight, in black and inky mantle. Ah, what wretch! To choose that most forbidding of hours—was I not blind?

Too late, now, to go back. I have begun to record the events, and I cannot stop before it's done.

The sun never rose that day; yet I, with blithe and elevated spirit, packed my haversack and made ready to spend the forenoon walking to the hills. By afternoon I should reach my uncle's home, and there I'd stay the night, and go hunting with him the following morn. I never made it to that hunt.

It began with the leaves across my path, skittering like horrid spiders on clackity legs. I beheld that they came only from the east, though the wind seemed to buffet me this way and that, laying a harsh blow upon my face no matter where I turned. Undeterred, young as I was, I merely tugged my collar up to settle more snugly around my neck, and forged on, humming to myself above the building gale.

Not far into the darkling morn, I reached those dense woods that squat about the base of hills, draping their branches upon their neighbors like drunken fellows. They stumbled up the incline in uneven rows, and in daylight, I was able to see the unsteadiest members fallen to the earth, branching coattails sprawled in inebriated disgrace. I was in the habit of looking upon those unhappy revellers and seeing in their rotting forms and peeling bark a keen commentary on the brevity of life; but on that morning, I could see nothing past a half dozen steps at a time, and the woods were so impregnably black, it might have been midnight in Alaskan winter.

Oh, if I had but meditated on the tenuous nature of life that day, and turned back before it was too late! But I was a stalwart young man, afraid of nothing, with a mind so honed in logic that it could summon no fancies to inhabit the solemn darkness. Resettling my haversack I forged on into the sober woods, leaves slithering across my path, and the wind ever worsening, so that when I stepped beneath the emaciated trees I was caught in a veritable storm of air, my breath snatched away without preamble. I looked up in awe—aye, not fear, so help my soul—to behold the spindly arms of those drunken revellers sweeping and dancing against the near-black sky, though it was not yet noon, and their violent movement bespoke to me a kind of poetry; so I stood, mesmerised, feeling the beating of the winter wind against my back, cutting away snatches of breath to fuel its fury. And I was not afraid, but fancied I heard a meditative rumble, like distant thunder echoing through the midnight woods. It occurred to me that such a purr might herald a storm, but I calculated that I would be well nigh to my uncle's house before any such tumult might strike

—so I was as yet unperturbed.

When I had stood for a time beneath that maelstrom of branches, whistling and striking one another in violent melee, I lowered my face, kicked away some leaves that had sought refuge about my feet, quivering against the persistent eastern force that drove them ever across my path, and made ready to continue. The day was now very dark indeed, and it occurred to me that mayhap the night would come earlier than I predicted. And so, with a sense of practical—yet not desperate—urgency, I set off again at a quickened pace.

Each stride brought harsher winds, and now the leaves were so copious about my feet that I was accompanied every step by a clamour of scratching and crumbling, until I fancied I was wading through bones, rather than leaves. The darkness was so absolute that I found I could not longer see the path I followed, and was surprised when I wandered too far to one side or the other, encountering a looming trunk. Many times, I put my hand out and touched the bark before I stumbled headlong into the skeletal tree—and I was amazed to find the rough surface studded and pockmarked with sores, as if some acid had been thrown against it. Each and every tree I encountered this way was so marked, and I began then to wonder at my situation. I could see little, and navigated primarily through the senses of my feet and outstretched arms, like a man blind and deaf—for the gale was so strong about me that I could hear naught but the hissing of the leaves, and the moaning of the trees as they tossed their heads to the storm. And ever present below all these sounds was the rumbling: like thunder, or perhaps a great engine. It neither faded nor grew, but lingered on the edge of sensation.

When the ground began to slope gently upwards, I knew I had reached the proper hills, and I quickened my pace further, now concerned for my well being should this unnatural storm grow any worse. I anticipated rain, but found the air coarse and dry against my face, scrubbing my eyes of tears as it burst upon me in spurts of violent energy.

I was increasingly worried for my situation, and when an especially strong burst brought what I suppose must have been a substantial branch—mayhap a whole tree—down in the woods someplace to my left, I threw caution to the biting wind, and ran. Forgetting my comfort in these Janus woods, I ran and ran, my legs entangled in leaves, my arms propelling me as I ricocheted from tree to dissuading tree. I fancied those ageing sores I felt infecting my own palms, and I feared what I could not see, finding at last a cause for concern, as the welfare of my body was cast to unsound fortune.

I don't know how I managed to navigate those dour woods, but I burst at last upon open turf, and beheld the cottage of my uncle not twenty yards from where I stood. The little light of the overcast day was like a spotlight in my eyes, and I raised my right hand to shade them—only to find it rough and cold against my face. Confused, I lowered it and flexed my fingers, but they would not move, and my hand remained flush and slightly cupped, ready to hold some object I lacked.

As my eyes gradually recovered in the relative light of that darkest day, I beheld the truth with horror —my right hand was grown heavy and jagged with black and rotting bark, dotted with those self-same irregular marks I'd touched on every tree. I staggered in shock, raising my left hand to find the same terrible phenomenon—and at once the cacophony of noise that had pursued me through the woods rose up like a terrible wave, building to such intensity that I swore it spoke words, though I did not know their language. Wind exploded from the east, and I turned uselessly away as it blasted my back, bringing with it that inexhaustible army of dead leaves that had harassed me all my journey. But rather than passing me, as they had before, they caught on my clothes and wrapped about me, covering my legs and back before I could draw a fresh breath.

I was now in the throes of a horror I had never before dreamed; I had not believed it at first, but as I stood, paralyzed, feeling my joints freeze up in dreadful wooden prehension, the ubiquitous rumbling seized hold of me, and I knew it for what it was. The vast network of trees, the host of roots, branches, trunks—*I could hear them growing.* My feet were held fast in the ground, and I could hardly turn my head to see the looming shadow of those woods, darkening, thickening overhead. It was not natural, the speed at which those woods stretched towards me, overtaking the small space of open ground I had barely gained before my arrest. I knew that it was coming for me, and should I harbour any hopes in making it through this night of day, I needed to find my strength and break the paralysis that seized my form. All thoughts of visiting my uncle were gone, and as leaves curled across my face, I no longer knew the direction in which his welcoming house lay.

A sudden, unearthly screech broke the air, shredding the rasping leaves that coated my ears. Freed by such a sound, I snapped my feet from clinging tendrils that threatened to bind me in place forever. It was the screeching of the woods giving pursuit, I thought, and ran as fast as I could, burdened by a shell of bark and leaf still clinging to my body.

Somehow I managed to find open ground again, and at last the form of my uncle's house, which I made my destination, intent on warning him of the imminent danger. But I was swiftly overtaken by shadow, and felt the snaps of branches all around, snatching at my hair and unnaturally changed body. I gasped as the wind propelled me along with this nightmare, the ground torn asunder by restless roots, and the angry rumbling of a thousand thirsting beasts pounding in my chest.

My uncle's house was enveloped in bark and leaf, the faint light in the windows snuffed out. In a clamour of leaves I found myself running down out of the hills, at the northern end of the territory. A spark of recognition came with an old, browbeaten sign signifying the way to a small town, where my uncle would fain get the few necessities he needed to live. I stumbled across the frozen ground, praying for a morning to end this night—though I knew it must still be afternoon, and true night was yet to come. This knowledge was coal laid on the fire of my fear, and I pressed on, spurred by terror of what may yet pursue me.

Through some miracle of fortune, I reached the small settlement with no further molestation and found my way to a shop of convenience. What a sight I was, when I entered that fair establishment! My face was scratched and raw; my hands—thank God, they were no longer entrapped as I had seen, but rather scraped and chapped to some bloody degree; my clothes were stuck with twigs and clinging leaves, spattered with earth and soiled with some stinking pitch. I was a certain spectacle to the poor man who ran the shop, but he gladly gave his help, and I was able to clean up to some degree, and stay with him and his wife for the night.

I did not think for a moment that I was free from danger. All through the night, the wind raged, and leaves tapped ever against the window near where I lay wrapped in insomnia. The rumbling was there at the back of my senses and touched my spine with fever chills until the creeping and hesitant light of dawn at last liberated me. It was with dumb disbelief that I beheld a normal day to follow that horror, and I stayed but a short time in town before purchasing passage on a coach, taking the south road around the hills back to my home. I could not bear to traverse those hills again. Perched in fear, I rode past their brooding forms in silent horror, until at last I was returned to surroundings familiar to me.

In the nearly ten years that have followed that night, I never glimpsed more motion from those woods. But when the perishing season comes, and the leaves drop from the trees, I shy away from their brittle bodies. And when the shadows are lengthening, and day mimics night to perfection, I hear the rumbling of those miserable woods, and I wonder —what wretch has been caught to stand among their ranks?

Catherine McCarthy

Curio

WAS HIS FIRST BORN.

I still recall the words my father spoke as my lungs inflated with air and I gasped my first breath. "My child," he said. "My little miracle." His eyes welled with tears of pride. "Come…see. I have made a special home for you where you will be safe. It even has its own garden." He held my naked form in cupped hands and carried me over to the countertop which ran around the perimeter of the room. And his eyes never left my face. Not once.

Father set me down upon a circular board lined with a bed of dried grass, and propped my spine against a small, crimson-leafed maple, sculpted from the real thing. He placed a glass dome over the top and stepped back to admire his handiwork. "There," he said, grinning from ear to ear. "Aren't you something special? We'll make many a sovereign, you and I." The workshop was bitterly cold, and as he spoke his stagnant breath clouded the glass.

As the condensation cleared, I saw my reflection for the first time. There, grotesquely magnified by the curve of the dome, was the head of a tiny infant. Narrow eyes, puffy and expressionless, nestled in mottled skin, the colour of dried lavender. Gaping nostrils flared and narrowed to the rhythm of my breathing, whilst flaking lips, tinted blue, struck a horizontal line.

Father continued to watch as I took in the spectacle that was me. Of course, I did not yet think of him as Father. In fact I thought very little, for in those first minutes I was barely cognizant. And yet, with each lungful of air, awareness of my surroundings grew.

Around my throat I wore a necklace of cross stitches, sewn from the thread of horse hair and caked with dark, dried blood.

But my chest was magnificent! Arrow-shaped feathers, in shades of bronze and sepia, nestled amongst a background of pure white down. I later learned that Father had endowed me with the body of a tawny owl. He'd clipped its wings, though. He would never allow me to fly. He had also chosen not to provide me with legs, unlike some of my siblings who came later.

For several minutes Father and I studied each other, unblinking. Beneath small, round spectacles, his pupils shone wide with excitement, and his scleras were interlaced with bloody tributaries. A toothless grin sat below a salt and pepper moustache which was yellowed with tobacco stains. Sprouting beneath a cap, an abundance of snowy white hair waved in all directions.

Eventually he spoke. "We must name you," he said, in a voice cracked with emotion, "but I shall need to give the matter some consideration."

Before he retired for the night, Father placed my bell jar on a high shelf so that I gained a bird's eye view of the workshop.

To my right, in a glass specimen jar, floated the trunk and limbs of a new-born baby boy. Suspended in formaldehyde, it wasn't until much later that I realized it once belonged to me. To my left, and in a similar jar, the large round eyes of a tawny owl stared in shock.

From this elevated position I took in my surroundings: a cluttered industrial room, with high beamed ceiling, brick walls, and bare floorboards. Wooden shelves were stacked with old books and all manner of bottles and jars, labelled in Latin. Around the perimeter of the room ran a narrow countertop littered with hand-written notes and diagrams, animal hides, and bones. I studied the implements on the workbench at the centre of the room, the one upon which I was born: bloody knives and scalpels, tweezers, needles and threads were strewn haphazardly—a murder scene in miniature. Or was it? For Father had brought forth new life from the carcasses of the dead.

Around the room, his most prized works of art were displayed in glass cases and domes: a red fox wore a hide of peacock feathers; a white mouse, carrying a tiny tea tray, stood on hind legs; a ginger kitten, with the wings of a dove, was suspended from wire as if in flight. I watched them closely for signs of life, though none so much as flexed a muscle.

I later learned they were his practice pieces. Only after Father had made his pact with the dark stranger was he granted the ability to breathe life into another.

On the second day Father woke me early, before the sun had risen. He appeared anxious, but once he was certain I had survived the night he calmed. As he removed the glass dome, I scrutinised his face without the distorted magnification of the concave glass. His frown of concern eased as he examined my neck wound.

"Knitting together just fine," he said. "Your head must be able to follow the gaze of your audience. When these stitches heal, you will be able to rotate two hundred and seventy degrees through the neck without breaking blood vessels or tearing tendons. What a spectacle you'll make!" His eyes glinted like jewels as he spoke.

The very next day, the travelling freak show came to town.

In preparation, Father carefully boxed and loaded

his prize specimens into the back of a little wagon. Last but not least, I joined them. Father packed the space around my bell jar tight with straw, thus shrouding my vision. Having harnessed the horse, we set off. After a while, the rhythmic clip clop of the mare's hooves lulled me to sleep.

Before long we reached the town square, and I heard Father whoa the horse. Having set up his display, Father gathered his fellow friends and gave them the spiel about how he had created a new freak of nature. "Are you ready to see?" he said, before whisking away a drape of red velvet which had thus far concealed me from prying eyes. As I blinked into sudden daylight, an audible gasp rose from the onlookers.

There in front of me stood a young woman with asymmetric features and a puzzled expression. Her wide mouth gaped open, displaying two enormous front teeth which were out of proportion to the rest of her face. Strangest of all was the top of her head, for its conical crown, shaved close to the skull, appeared to belong to a different person, someone much smaller or younger.

Looming over her, in stark contrast, stood a giant of a man, so tall his shoulders extinguished the sun, or so it seemed.

The girl with the conical head spoke, and despite my lack of experience, her words and tone were all wrong—mouse-like and nonsensical.

"Is it another of your taxidermy stunts?" a gruff

female voice called from the rear of the crowd.

"Come, see for yourself," Father replied. His expression was one of sheer joy as a rotund woman, scantily dressed in vivid red, jostled her way to the front. She bent down to get a closer look, and as she did so, oozing rolls of fat escaped her clothing. As I rotated my neck a half turn, the audience gasped as one.

"It's a trick!" someone cried.

"Some kind of automaton," shouted another.

But the fat lady knew what she had witnessed —the head of a new-born infant, upon the torso of an owl, had turned its face away from her. "Aren't you kinda sweet?" she said, and the distorted image of her heavily made-up features reflected inside the glass surface of the bell jar. Her smile was wide, but I recognized the sadness in her eyes.

Moments later, the booming voice of the showman called everyone to order and I was whisked away until it was my turn to be leered at by a paying public. My heart raced as I awaited my destiny.

It has to be said, the showman did an excellent job of building up the crowd. His tone was majestic, imposing, and his lurid vocabulary and enticing phraseology whipped them into a frenzy. One by one, or in the case of the Siamese twins, two by two, the living exhibits were paraded before the insatiable audience. Hirsute ladies, a child with neither arms nor legs, and middle-age men, no taller than my display table, took turns at being ridiculed.

And it seemed I was the only living creature

amongst them to be sickened by the spectacle. The only one who saw through the cracks, the grinning veneer.

And my tiny heart bled.

All too soon the spotlight shone on me. A thousand faces, or so it seemed, took turns to gaze into my house of glass. Each face magnified and distorted into a living nightmare. Each shriek of laughter, each cry of horror muffled by the glass, reminding me of the moment of my birth as the chloroform wore off. The memory of its sickly-sweet smell, accompanied by a profound sense of confusion, came flooding back until I thought I might vomit. But even if I had wanted to I would not have been able, for Father's alchemy dictated precisely which movements were and were not possible.

Soon I was exhausted. The stitches in my neck pulled and my throat was parched with passion.

As to the secrets of his trickery? Of course, Father gave little away. Instead he soaked up the lurid attention like a beggar did cheap gin.

As evening fell, the crowd dwindled. Father collected five shiny shillings from the showman and we set off home.

Exhausted from all the attention, and desperate to be reacquainted with the relative peace of the workshop, I was rather disappointed when Father pulled up the wagon shortly after leaving the fair. Boxed and blinded by straw packaging, I saw nothing, though to some degree I was still able to hear.

Judging by the echo of the horse's hooves, I imagined Father must have turned down some kind of narrow alleyway. He pulled the mare to a halt. Soon the sound of hobnail boots approached, followed by a short exchange between Father and another man who spoke in a hushed tone. The door of the wagon opened briefly, and a box of some sort was placed on the floor. The clink of coins announced an end to the illicit meeting.

The following morning, Father created my brother.

From my viewing platform on the shelf above his workbench, I watched with fascination as Father laboured, his aged hands as supple as a child's and his eyesight as keen as a hawk. Unusual, I thought, for one so elderly, but later, having learned of his pact with the dark stranger, it no longer surprised me.

The sweet, pungent smell of turpentine and tanning oil permeated even through the miniscule amount of air space between my baseboard and glass dome.

And Father was in his element.

Not one for waste, he amputated the tiny feet from what remained of my carcass and attached them to the front legs of a headless hare, leaving its hind legs intact. The head of a badger, with its distinctive black and white stripes, replaced that of the hare. Finally, he reattached the hare's long ears.

Glancing in my direction Father said, "Have no fear, little one. You shall be the only one capable of human thought and emotion, for it is you who received the human brain." At the time, his words made little sense. It was much later, and after being subjected to the cruel scrutiny of humans, that I understood their true impact. And it was then I wished I had never been born.

Oh, cruel world! Why does mankind find it necessary to gawk and thrill at those who bear the mark of difference?

I would grow to envy my badger-brother's lack of sentiment, as I would those who came later, though they too suffered the impediment of confinement.

I will never forget Father's next act, for it was the first time I witnessed such alchemy.

As my brother lay prone upon the bench, Father took an intricately carved, spouted cup from a locked cupboard and breathed into it, long and deep. Inserting the spout between my brother's dark lips, he tipped the cup backwards, at the same time reciting words in a foreign tongue. Within moments, my brother took his first breath and opened his eyes. Father cooed over him for a short while, before placing him inside a glass dome not dissimilar to my own. Of course, the same sorcery had been cast on me, though I had no recollection of it.

It dawned on me later, after Father had created three more siblings, that through his alchemy not only did he create life, but he also controlled its limits. My brother, fashioned from badger and hare, was able to move only his ears. Hearing was his most acute sense, so when spectators viewed him within the dome, his ears would twitch and stand erect at the slightest change in sound, resulting in shrieks of laughter.

One of my sisters received the nose of a black bear, set within the face of a fox. She therefore inherited an acute olfactory system, and thus was constantly hungry, though rarely fed. Which brings me to the matter of sister, for the felonious exchange that had occurred between Father and the man in the alleyway was the trading of a human corpse for a coin. Stillborn, though nonetheless illegally purchased, I began to understand that Father was procuring dead infants so that he might experiment with what he called, *his marvellous children.*

The carcasses of birds, reptiles, and mammals he either sourced himself or through his acquaintance with a local poacher.

As Father grew more confident in his work, his skills became more adept, until he was able to adorn his creations with minutiae detail, such as attaching the curled eyelashes of a cow to the head of a grass snake, and gifting it the power to flutter its wares at gentlemen observers.

On one occasion, he encrusted the chest of a

falcon with live snails which peeped from their coiled shells in tune to Father's harmonica.

As his living curios became more and more famous, Father grew wealthier, and thus was able to afford more exotic birds and animals from far-off shores.

He stuck to his word, though. Never again did he grant a creature the brain of a human.

Of course by now my own trick of being able to follow the gaze of admirers had worn off in comparison to the new delights Father had up his sleeve. Truth be told, he grew bored of me, sometimes forgetting I had not been fed, or that my dome had not been cleaned for several days, until the acrid stink of my own excrement burned my nostrils.

And he never did name me.

It was around the same time as the procurement of the tiger carcass that things began to turn especially grim. By then Father was intoxicated by his success, thrilled with each new addition to what he termed, *the family*. He'd grown affluent, infamous, and had no need to work any longer. But we had become his fix, his drug of choice, and he was neither willing nor able to relinquish the reins on his power over mortality.

Of course, the unsuspecting population assumed his works of art to be some kind of clever trickery or puppetry of sorts. Rumours whispered behind closed doors, eyebrows were raised and elbows prodded, though nothing came of it. Father was even questioned by the peelers, though he managed to charm them with his guile.

Then, one day, shortly after midsummer's eve, Father brought home a live one.

A cry of hunger reverberated around the workshop as he lifted its naked form from the swaddling. It lay on the cold workbench, angry and alert, legs kicking and fists crammed into its mouth. I watched helplessly from my perch, heart racing, as he selected the sharpest scalpel from a leather roll.

Licking his lips, he made the first incision, and I squeezed my eyes shut tight, wishing I had hands to cover my ears against the unholy scream.

A sudden blinding light pierced my lids, and the room was filled with the roar of one incensed. The flash of light abated, and I peered into the gloom towards the only Father I had ever known. And I smelled his fear.

Drained of life blood, the infant's cry ceased. Father held the scalpel aloft, whilst blood dripped onto the abdomen of the tiny corpse. Father's face froze in shock at the sight of the tall, dark being who towered over him. I saw in Father a moment of recognition and understood this was not the first time the two had met.

The stranger spoke, and in doing so a conflagration of flames spewed from his mouth, singeing Father's face and causing him to cry out in pain. "This was not part of the bargain," the stranger said, gesturing towards the prone body of the infant. "You have grown greedy and lustful and hence you shall be punished."

Father did not reply, for his pain was too intense.

"We made a pact which gave you power to re-animate the deceased, not to take the life of the innocent."

And with that, he wrapped a cape of burning wings around my Father, consuming him in flames, until he was no more than dust.

~~~

The dark stranger, face stern, visits each of my siblings in turn, contemplating the complexity of our assembled components. His fury at Father's atrocities, evident. He reaches for me, and his expression changes to one of empathy, for reflected in each other's eyes we recognize something of ourselves. Both of us bear the burden of difference.

I cannot say what will become of me and my siblings. Perhaps he will put an end to our misery. I am certain of one thing, though. I wish for this cruel carnival to end, that one day the people of this world will embrace difference with open arms and warm hearts instead of jibes and ridicule. Let that be my legacy.

James Dorr

Appointment
in Time

HE **ENGLISHMAN** was shown to the chair, the first of four he would sit in that day. This one, more a wide bench really, he shared with his escort, two members of the 17th Fusiliers in full dress uniform despite the beastly heat—even on the last day of December! He, a civilian, wore a black morning coat buttoned over a pale yellow waistcoat, grey wool pinstriped trousers, a starched white shirt and a Windsor tie, with polished boots, lavender gloves, and a tall-crowned bowler completing his attire. This was, after all, not England he found himself in, where full formal evening wear might have been called for.

He had, however, been chosen in England for the important role he was to play before he had even boarded the steamship out, a special arrangement commemorating the love that remained, the continuation of British ways, even though the land he was in now no longer retained its colonial status. It was out of this love, as that between a now grown child and its parent, that the ceremony continued virtually unchanged, just as it had from the earliest times, to guarantee prosperity for the year to come for what remained of a once far-flung empire. And it was only in this land that it could be conducted, with its unique mix of ancient gods and shamanistic culture alongside the modern customs of the West—the latter exemplified by the high clock tower they had even now started to ascend.

One of the soldiers, their uniforms modeled on those of the British they'd recently replaced, steadied the Englishman as the chair left the ground. "You be okay, Sir?" he asked.

The Englishman looked up first, craning his neck, to see the first puffs of steam high in the air from the vents in the roof above the great clock face. He nodded, yes. He could not show nervousness even though they were fifty feet over the plaza already, even now beginning, before the sun had fully set, to attract the vanguard of what would soon be throngs of celebrants, shoulder to shoulder, packing the square.

Stiff upper lip, he thought. England expects. He hadn't exactly volunteered for what was to happen, but as a member of the foreign service he had known that, any year, he could be the one chosen to represent the erstwhile mother country.

It was what he had been trained for, in a way. With everything else. That he had been unmarried was a factor also, allowing him more freedom when he arrived, for evenings in the capital city's less sedate sectors. For drinking. For love. For civilized pleasures as well as those less so.

But what was civilization, he thought, except accommodation for that which was needed, even if not fully understood. To acquiesce to the local culture, even while representing his own.

The best of both worlds, yes?

Still lost in his thoughts, he felt the sudden rise as the troopers on either side stood. They were on the first ledge. "Help you, sir?" one said as he stood up too, then let himself be led—glancing once back and down, toward the increasing crowd—through the narrow door into the tower's clockwork filled interior.

Here the Englishman was led between the great twin boilers that powered the mechanisms above them. The tower was still lighted, the last rays of the sun shining in through open louvres that pierced its walls. He climbed the metal stairs up to the catwalk that wound around and, in some cases, through the slowly turning gear train from flywheel to axle to crankshaft to belt to the central arbor that turned the clock's hands, so high above and lost in shadow that he had to strain his eyes to make it out.

"This way, Sir," a new voice said, breaking into the Englishman's thoughts. He had to admit what he was seeing was impressive! He allowed this new person, wearing the goggles and white pressed duster of a clock mechanic, to strap him into a second chair, one he would ride alone up past the pendulum chamber with its verge and crown wheel, its own gear train regulating the power train he had just viewed. And above it, the gong that sounded the hours, especially the twelve chimes that would sound at midnight, signifying the turning of the year. And, above *that,* the glint of more metal, of more machinery again hooked to pendulum and power train, to arbor and gong, for the culmination of this, the final day of December.

The technician handed the Englishman a bottle before he released the chair for its trip up. "To show our appreciation, Sir," he said. "It's imported Scotch whisky, from your own country. A man above will help you to a table and chair, where you can enjoy it, along with ice. Or seltzer, if you prefer. There'll be a light supper too."

The Englishman thanked him. He rode the chair up, then, noting how surprisingly fast it went, wondering if it, too, was connected to the main works of the clock, through yet one more gear train, or if it just had its own belt and flywheel independently taking it up and down as needed.

The chair finally stopped, hundreds of feet above where it had started, letting him off on a rough plank floor, with a crimson carpet muting its starkness. A man in a butler's livery appeared, ironically dressed in more formal style than the Englishman himself, in a swallow-tailed coat and linen shirt with a standing collar. A second servant, head bowed, stood behind him.

The butler led the Englishman to the third chair he would sit in, this one with a comfortably padded seat and back. "Please relax as much as you can, Sir," he said. "I and my colleague are here to serve you, in any way that we can, until it's time to go outside."

It was at this point the Englishman balked, if just for a moment. No, he thought. He made to turn back, to find a staircase, a ladder, anything leading down. It was all a horrible farce! But then he looked at the butler again, the calm determination on that man's face as he nodded to his assistant.

The Englishman nodded too. What was, was, he thought as the second servant brought up a small table with a single place setting, bringing as well a bottle of water and several dishes. They left the Englishman then to his own meditations until, several hours later, they returned to lead him outside to the ledge beneath the huge clock itself.

The Englishman was tipsy by then, feeling little pain as the butler handed him a snifter. "A special drink, Sir," he said. "Once more to show our appreciation —all England's appreciation, as well as those of us once in its family. You know what you must expect, I trust?"

The Englishman nodded. He drank down the brandy—if he had almost had second thoughts before, it was certainly too late now. The under servant strapped him into a chair—the fourth chair that evening—that was bolted to the stone ledge it stood on.

"It wouldn't do if you were to fall," he said.

"No," the Englishman said, "it would certainly not." He gazed out into the night, drinking in the square below, now packed with cheering men and women, their eyes looking up to him. Behind him he heard the click of turning gears.

Looking up briefly, he saw the clock's longer hand climbing to meet the hour hand at twelve. He heard the blood rushing through his veins and arteries—it was as if he had lived for this moment when all eyes were on him. When time *itself* seemingly depended on him.

And so, let it be, he thought. He heard another click, one more minute passed, then that drowned out by the beating of his heart. Everything concentrated on one thing, the necessary. The pre-appointed. That which must be.

He felt a stirring in his stomach as, with a reverberating *clang!,* the first stroke of the hour of midnight chimed. Driving out all other sound as spider-hands, made of articulated brass, reached out from a door in the clock face behind him and gripped him fast in the confines of his chair. With the second chime other hands reached out, divesting him of his coat and outer clothes, tattering, ripping the fabric from him. Letting it drift to the crowd beneath as, on the third chime, knife blades appeared to glint in the searchlights that trained on him from below.

He felt no pain—he was caught in the moment. Destiny could not be stopped in any event as the fourth gong sounded, starting the carving. Fifth, sixth, seventh, eighth, with each of these strokes of approaching midnight an arm or a leg was torn from his body and let fall below. With the ninth chime more blades appeared as the crowd roared louder, those that had already done their work retreating back into the great clock's interior, and with the tenth his gut was slit open, letting his entrails unfold themselves in his lap.

Two chimes to go.

And with the eleventh the flaying commenced, and with it the cutting off of his head, while, with what was left of his body slumped, still strapped in its chair, more stirrings began. The crowd fell to silence. Sprawled on its narrow seat, the Englishman's limbless corpse trembled as the final, twelfth stroke rang—and, scratching, clawing its way through blood and flesh, shakily standing, the New Year came forth.

CONTRIBUTORS

JOHN ADAMS (he/him/his) writes stories and plays about teenage detectives, robo-butlers, and cursed cowboys in a genre he's coined "absurdist speculative melodrama"—meaning "monsters being monstrous, aliens being alien, and humans being all too painfully human." He performs with THAT'S NO MOVIE, a multigenre improv team.

Web:
JohnAmusesNoOne.com
Twitter:
@JohnAmusesNoOne

DEBORAH L. DAVITT was raised in Nevada, but lives in Houston, Texas with her husband and son. She's known for her Pushcart-nominated poetry, short stories, and novels. Her work has appeared in *F&SF* and *Asimov's* among other venues. For more about her work, please see

Edda-Earth.com
/bibliography

JAMES DORR works mostly in dark fantasy/horror with some forays into science fiction and mystery. His *The Tears of Isis* was a 2013 Stoker finalist for Superior Achievement in a Fiction Collection, while his latest book is a novel-in-stories, *Tombs: A Chronicle of Latter-Day Times of Earth,* published by Elder Signs Press. He has also been a technical writer, an editor on a regional magazine, a full time non-fiction freelancer, and a semi-professional musician, and currently harbors a Goth cat named Triana.

JamesDorrWriter
.wordpress.com

JONATHAN LOUIS DUCKWORTH is a completely normal, entirely human person with the right number of heads and everything. He received his MFA from Florida International University. His speculative fiction work appears in *Pseudopod, Beneath Ceaseless Skies, Southwest Review, Tales to Terrify, Flash Fiction Online,* and elsewhere. He is a PhD student at University of North Texas and an active HWA member.

DIANA A. HART lives in Washington State, speaks fluent dog, and escapes whenever somebody leaves the gate open —if lost, she can be found rolling dice at the closest table-top game store. Her passion for storytelling stems from a well-used library card and years immersed in the oral traditions of the Navajo.

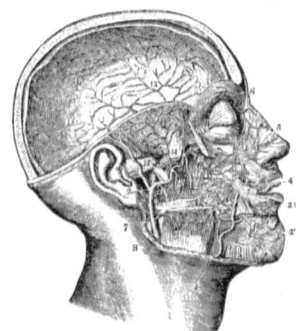

LIAM HOGAN is an award winning short story writer, with stories in *Best of British Science Fiction* 2016 & 2019, and *Best of British Fantasy* 2018 (NewCon Press). He's been published by *Analog, Daily Science Fiction,* and Flame Tree Press, among others. He helps host Liars' League London, volunteers at the creative writing charity Ministry of Stories, and lives and avoids work in London. More details at

HappyEnding
NotGuaranteed
.blogspot.co.uk

RESTORE YOUR SIGHT !

TOSHIYA KAMEI holds an MFA in Literary Translation from the University of Arkansas. His translations have appeared in such venues as *Clarkesworld, The Magazine of Fantasy & Science Fiction,* and *Strange Horizons.*

ELAINE VILAR MADRUGA is a Cuban poet, fiction writer, and playwright whose work has appeared in numerous literary journals and anthologies around the globe. She has authored more than thirty books, most recently *Los años del silencio* (2019). Translated

by Toshiya Kamei, Elaine's short fiction and poetry have appeared in venues such as *The Magazine of Fantasy & Science Fiction, Star*Line,* and *World Literature Today.*

---◆---

THIS TOO

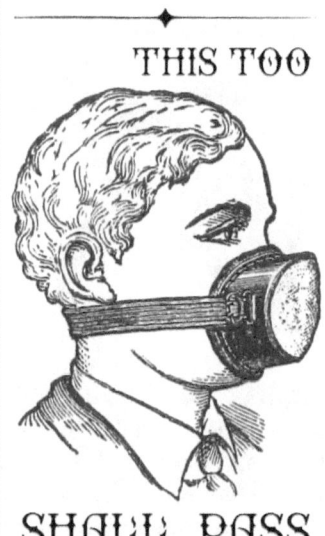

SHALL PASS

---◆---

BOGDAN MARICA is a Romanian digital artist working in the video games industry. Over the years he has contributed to a multitude of projects for different game companies such as Ubisoft, Bioware, Ready at Dawn and many others, where he has created enviroment concept art, character designs and marketing illustrations. You can find out more about his work at

bogdanmrk.com

---◆---

CATHERINE MCCARTHY is a Welsh author of dark tales with macabre melodies. She is the author of the short story collection, *Mists and Megaliths,* and *Immortelle,* a novella published by Off Limits Press in July 2021. When she is not writing she may be found hiking the Welsh coast path or huddled among ancient gravestones reading Machen or Poe. Discover more at

catherine-mccarthy-author.com

ANDREW MCCURDY is a writer and editor whose day job as a Speech-Language Pathologist involves helping nonverbal children access technology to help them communicate. He lives in rural Nova Scotia with his daughter, two immortal cats, and an assortment of feral creatures who have taken over ownership of the woodshed and only grant access if he's carrying food.

LENA NG skulks around Toronto, Canada, and is a zombie member of the Horror Writers Association. She tiptoes at night so no one knows she's awake. *Under an Autumn Moon* is her short story collection. She is currently seeking a publisher for her novel, *Darkness Beckons,* a Gothic romance.

"Let's make a deal!"

◆

Thank you slushers: Irene Puntí, Lori Alden Holuta, & Serafina Puchkina. If you would like to join the jolly reading crew on a future Curiosities submission session, contact Kevin Frost at CuriousGallery@gmail.com

MARISCA PICHETTE is a bisexual author of speculative fiction, poetry, and essay, living in Western Massachusetts. More of her work can be found in *Strange Horizons, PseudoPod, Grimdark Magazine,* and *Uncharted,* among others She is on Twitter as

@MariscaPichette

◆

MARY SANGIOVANNI is an award winning horror/thriller writer of novels, novellas, short stories, comics, and nonfiction. She has an MA in Writing Popular Fiction from Seton Hill University. She was a co-host on *The Horror Show with Brian Keene,* is a current co-host of *The Ghostwriters Podcast,* and hosts her own podcast on cosmic horror, *Cosmic Shenanigans.*

ALLEN'S LUNG BALSAM

To stay up to date on our reading sessions, podcasts, and print & ebook releases, visit the Curiosities homepage at GalleryCurious.com, *or follow us on Twitter* @GalleryCurious